I0771176

SNAPPER

SNAPPER

A NOVEL

PETE MECCA

DEEDS PUBLISHING | ATHENS

Published by Deeds Publishing in Athens, GA
www.deedspublishing.com

Printed in The United States of America

Cover and interior design by Deeds Publishing

ISBN 978-1-961505-49-0

Books are available in quantity for promotional or premium use. For information, email info@deedspublishing.com.

First Edition, 2025

10 9 8 7 6 5 4 3 2 1

I made it home.
58,281 of my brothers and sisters did not.
Their names are on a long black granite wall.
This book is dedicated to their memory.
Rest in peace. A job well done.

CHAPTER ONE:
THE AFRICAN ORPHAN

The oldest earth layers, called cratons, theoretically began the formation of primordial supercontinents. Geologists speculate the Kaapval and Pilbara cratons came together in a less-than-happy marriage around three or four billion years ago to form the first supercontinent called Vaalbara. After ten million years of ecological and violent volcanic territorial disputes, Vaalbara's offspring, Kaapval and Pilbara, detached from Vaalbara to form another supercontinent called Ur. After Ur, came Kenorland, eventually to be replaced by Columbia, then Rodinia, until the creation of the undisputed Big Momma supercontinent called Pangea along with one of its scions called Gondwanaland.

Dinosaurs emerged on Pangea around 250 million years ago, as did the first known species of turtle. As life thrived, so did the movement of global plate tectonics. One hundred and eighty million years later, give or take a few million years, the eastern part of Gondwanaland separated into the future continents of Arabia, Africa, Madagascar, India, Australia, and

Antarctica. India shed Madagascar and eventually slammed into Eurasia with enough muscle to create the Himalayan Mountain Range.

Arabia didn't advance very far but hoarded the debris of dead organisms until fuel-starved populations began drilling for oil. Antarctica journeyed southward to chillier surroundings with subzero temperatures. Australia trekked further eastward in the direction of the Southeast Asia continent and continues its journey to this day, meaning, in a few billion years down under will be up yonder.

As Pangea came apart, its progeny, Gondwanaland, continued its destruction. The dinosaurs (and turtles) drifted westward on a chunk of terrain later identified as North and South America with an attachment destined to evolve into a tropical vacation utopia and lucrative tourist trap called Florida.

What remained of Gondwanaland attached to North America as the remnants of Pangea crept westward to form continents and long chains of sultry islands whose names became household words during WWII. Back east, South America broke away and moved south to develop into banana republics, cocaine capitols, and a petite sliver of land the human species would eventually dredge up to connect two oceans.

Florida rejected the idea of moving south and

remained glued to North America to continue her birthing, but the delivery would be grueling.

Florida slipped under the ocean to become part of the North American continental shelf. Thus began her formation into a limestone foundation as crustaceans, coral, fish skeletons, dead and dying organisms, fecal matter, and the residue of aquatic lifecycles filtered to the bottom to create layers of limestone hundreds and thousands of feet thick. Florida's growth was a see-saw affair, emerging and submerging at least four times from beneath the waves. During one breakout to daylight, Florida's western coastline extended over a hundred miles into the Gulf of Mexico, or the Gulf of America, take your pick.

Above water, eroding rocks from the Appalachian Mountains, at one time as prominent as the Himalayas, dumped quartz sand and clay over Florida's limestone. Florida, nonetheless, remained addicted to salt-life and spent most of her existence under the ocean, and to the ocean, Florida may one day return. With her highest elevation at a breathtaking 320 feet, another dunk in the ocean is inevitable.

Present-day Florida is in relentless transformation, from human activity to the diverse wildlife to its thick limestone foundation relentlessly eroded by freshwater. No acreage is stable as the malleable limestone continues its unremitting dissolvent that honeycombs the state with profuse underground rivers,

rivers that breach the spongy surface to form sinkholes, marshlands, springs, everglades, and lakes, like
the organic lake behind Pete Colucci's property.

CHAPTER TWO:
THE REFUGE

Turtlezilla basked motionless on a far bank across the deep lake behind Pete Colucci's property. The snapping turtle's carapace approximated the size of a trash can lid, its leathery legs thick, the claws and jaws injurious to animal lovers careless enough to consider the creature for a pet. Pete nicknamed the Chelydra serpentina "Turtlezilla" due to its enormous size, the largest snapping turtle inhabiting the various man-made ponds or one of six larger, wider, and cavernous organic lakes of 'The Refuge' modular home community near the small township of New St. Francis, Florida.

The town had taken its name from the once palmy riverport city of St. Francis, now an isolated ghost town since the late 1800s after early train lines replaced steamboat traffic along the St. Johns River.

The Refuge was developed over the huge acreage of a drained swamp adjacent to the St. Johns River just north of Spuds and a few miles south of Molasses Junction. Although incorporated, New St. Francis numbered less than 2,000 residents and didn't even have enough political or business credentials to qual-ify for a Dollar General Store.

Digging potatoes in Spuds or harvesting the or-ange groves north of Molasses Junction were two sources of an irregular paycheck augmented by three or four less-than-thriving fishing and hunting enter-prises. A lone Marathon gas station still pumped fuel for customers, checked their tires, and washed wind-shields. The one bank wasn't worth robbing.

The peaceful nothingness of New St. Francis attracted retirees and prosperous families seeking a tropical Utopia, which brought a suitable amount of financial stability to the community. Good old boys thundered up and down the roads in paint-faded and rusting pickup trucks, yet one or two ostentatious new trucks often joined the daily rat race to nowhere.

The remoteness of the town also appealed to a class of laidback folks, yet northern snowbirds were rare. Confederate flags fluttering from several mobile homes, tailgates, and shabby fishing shacks contrib-uted to a snowbird's hesitancy to overstay their visit.

Like most of the swampy acreage around New St. Francis, The Refuge was home to several species of ducks, Canadian geese, fish, turtles, snakes, egrets, birds of every color and song, the Osceola wild turkey, and lonesome White-tailed stags sniffing for a doe.

Seven species of Florida hawks patrolled the skies, especially during duckling season, in search of a trouble-free meal. Newborn ducklings provided a quick snack for snakes, bobcats, feral cats, snapping turtles, and gators; every predator in the Sunshine State sought ducklings. A duckling's survival depended on sheer luck since a momma duck lacked offensive or defensive weapons.

Pete Colucci's home was not modular. Roughly ten percent of The Refuge's residents lived in 'stick built' homes on concrete slabs. The Homeowners Association wisely banned any crawl-space dwellings since the moist and semi-protective soil would offer a good hiding place or nesting habitat for any number of animals.

Pete's home was typical ranch style: three bedrooms, two full baths, a two-car garage, a kitchen, and a glass-enclosed sunroom accessible from the living room. The house sat on a half-acre of land, the ground squelchy after downpours or fried crispy during dry spells. An algae-stained six-foot-high white paneled fence enclosed the sides of the backyard with a chain-linked fence running across the back to offer a nice view of the lake, plus a gate for access.

Pete had arranged concrete pavers under a large acorn tree and up against the chain-linked fence to create the likeness of a small patio. Four old-fashioned red metal lawn chairs, faded by age and Florida sunshine, a routine residence for spiders, ants, and spattered with bird droppings, offered a lake view for anyone unconcerned about soiling their garb.

A cutie-pie neighbor occupied the modular home on the north side of Pete's property; the empty lot on the south side of his property was flat and void of vegetation, still up for sale.

Pete Colucci was fond of Rum and Dr. Pepper. Mixed with any flavor of Dr. Pepper or straight-up over ice, Pete spent many an afternoon under the acorn tree sipping booze while observing the wildlife he knew little about. A few pounds overweight for a 5'9" frame, Pete's olive skin, Roman nose, and Mediterranean sweat glandes that worked overtime in Florida's humidity gave away his Italian ancestry.

Like so many older males, Pete grew more hair out of his ears than his cranium. His wife had died of breast cancer over two years ago. After her death, Pete moved from Atlanta to New St. Frances to help care for his 90-year-old sister, who had recently passed from lung cancer. Pete loathed cancer. He donated to the American Cancer Society when Lady Luck massaged his leg at the new St. Augustine Best Bet Poker Room.

Pete loved poker. He applied his winnings to augment a social security check and a low-paying, intermittent newspaper article about veterans. The author of three obscure books on Amazon that earned a few bucks now and then, Pete generated more money hosting a weekly Zoom radio gig out of Pittsburgh or occasional patriotic speeches at American Legions and VFWs. Pete enjoyed poker, rum mixed with Dr. Pepper, advocated for veterans, and hated cancer. Such was his life.

His daughter, Lisa, had just turned forty, but still turned heads with a cute figure, long curly auburn hair, the face of an angel, and the personality of a comedian. She resembled her dad. He had jokingly threatened to disclaim Lisa on several occasions, but her reply was always the same, 'Good luck with that.'

Lisa had a degree in Chemistry, but being defiant and independent to the core, she refused corporate life. She spent as much time as possible in Florida with her dad after laboring seven days a week every week in Atlanta peddling a homespun offshoot of Viagra. Borderline legal, her product 'Stay Straight' produced an obscene income.

Divorced from her first husband, a young man Lisa said, 'never stayed straight', she was content playing the field, fully aware that the Field of Dreams with men didn't exist. To Lisa, a dude was a dude who thought with the wrong head. Thus, her prosperous business peddling 'Stay Straight' to wannabe studs. She was also a hell of a poker player. Such was her life.

Pete and his daughter wiped away the bird poot, a bevy of ants, and three small spiders; flopped down in two of the red metal lawn chairs, and poured them-selves a drink from a clear plastic pitcher filled with a concoction of Captain Morgan Spice Rum and the only soft drinks they found in the frig, Cream Soda Dr. Peppers, and shot the breeze in the summer breeze.

Pete wore baggy khaki shorts, a faded indigo T-shirt, and upscale flip-flops impersonating pricey sandals. His daughter's threadbare blue jeans covered most of her legs, and a pink Panama Jack T-shirt veiled her upper torso. She wore an in-vogue pair of sandals, unlike her father's upmarket flip-flops. Late afternoon, the sun slowly descending, yet Pete still wore his sun-glasses, the same pair he sported when playing poker.

Their three canines; Hank, a black and white Bos-ton Terrier; Cloe, a golden-blondish mutt of a hun-dred ancestries; and Lily, a nasty little bitch Chihua-hua, sat or laid on the patio's concrete pavers.

Lisa sipped the rum and pepper mixture. *Terrible,* she thought, turning up her nose reproachfully. "This crap tastes really bad, Dad," she complained.

Pete swigged rather than sipped, licked his lips then said, "Fine with me, Kido, that means more for me." Kido was his favorite nickname for Lisa; Pete rarely articulated her first name unless angered or in case of an emergency.

"Be my guest," she said, glancing at the lake. "The water is the lowest I've ever seen it. We could use a good rain."

Pete replied, "According to the Jacksonville weather heifer we are getting a hard rain in the morning. Maybe that will improve the water level and cool off things a bit."

"The weather heifer," Lisa repeated, smiling. "I like that. It's a good description of that woman. I bet she weighs two hundred pounds."

"She'll not be fighting off my sexual advances, that's for sure," Pete replied, snickering. "You still leaving in the morning if it's raining?"

"Yeah, I need to get back. Orders are piling up and I can't trust those young bozos I hired to hustle as they should."

Pete saw Turtlezilla move, then stop just as suddenly. "You see Turtlezilla over there taking his sunbath? I wonder if turtles use sunscreen?"

"Real funny, Dad," Lisa retorted. "I like turtles; Turtlezilla is the biggest one I've ever seen. What kind of turtle do you think it is?"

"He's a snapper," Pete said confidently.

Lisa looked at her dad. "How do you know it's a 'he'? Did you pick it up and look at his dinger?"

"Of course not," Pete replied, chuckling. "I looked up snapping turtles on Google and learned a little bit about them. Turtlezilla is a 'he' due to its size. Male snappers are larger than female snappers and that guy cooking his ass over there on the bank is a monster."

"I think he's cute," Lisa said, knocking back what

little remained of her rum and pepper. She grabbed the plastic pitcher to pour another full serving into a Red Solo cup. "We forgot to bring out ice," she complained, filling the cup.

"What do you need ice for?" Pete teased. "I thought you didn't like the rum and pepper."

"It grows on you," she replied, setting the pitcher back onto the white metal patio table.

Pete chortled again, then took another sizable swig of his rum and pepper as his gaze returned to the lake, a gaze partially blocked by over-hanging limbs on the Acorn tree. Pete seldom trimmed the over-hanging limbs since their sagging formed an umbrella-like shelter to shade his paver-built patio. The night was slowly approaching; the sun was fading behind red streaks in the western sky, visibility dwindling.

He noticed Turtlezilla moving backward. Pete had never seen the big turtle act in such an odd manner. Suddenly, something enormous emerged from the middle of the lake, apparently the head only, the size of a Volkswagen Beetle, then it submerged just as quickly. The three dogs noticed. Lily yapped twice, but Pete wasn't sure what he had seen. He leaned to his right for a better view. "What in God's name was that?" he said, removing his sunglasses.

"What?" Lisa said, glancing at the disturbed water in the middle of the lake. She noticed sizable water rings spreading out, took a quick gulp of rum and pepper, and then suggested, "Big fish, Dad."

"Big fish, my ass!" Pete said forcefully as he stood up, hoping to see what he had seen again. "Whatever that thing was could pass for a whale!"

"Oh, please," Lisa said, looking up at her dad. "How much have you had to drink?"

Pete's stare remained frozen on the water rings. "Not enough, I can tell you that!" He looked down at his daughter. "Kido, I'm serious, something big is out there, something… something big, it's gigantic!"

"Maybe it's a Russian submarine."

Pete was not amused. "That's not funny. I'm telling you, that thing out there isn't normal, it was… it was titanic!"

"Titanic," Lisa blandly repeated. "Well, there's your answer; it's a sunken ocean liner resurfacing." Lisa stood up, guzzled her drink, and then said, "That 'thing,' as you say, will probably be out there in the morning, so maybe you'll get to see it again. It's getting dark, Dad, and I'm hungry. Let's go to Outback over in St. Augustine."

Pete looked back at the lake. The ripples were fading, a calm returning to the lake. "Man, I don't know what that… well, to hell with it. Maybe somebody else will see it." He looked at his daughter and called to mind, "The dogs saw it."

Lisa wasn't impressed with canine eyewitnesses.

"Well, that's terrific, Dad. Dogs are always reliable witnesses," she replied, her tone condescending. She pointed at the back door to the sunroom and then instructed the dogs, "Let's go, guys." All three sprinted for the house. Lisa's attention returned to her father as his gaze refocused on the lake. "Forget it, Dad," she said. "Com'on, let's go."

"Fine," he replied, gathering the pitcher and unused solo cups before heading for the house. "I could use a drink."

"A drink?" Lisa retorted. "One more drink, and you'll imagine a Carnival cruise ship punching through the floor at Outback!"

"I haven't had that much to drink."

"Really? You just saw the Titanic resurface in the middle of the lake. I'd say that's the booze talking… or observing, take your pick."

"Give me a break," Pete said but rethought his condition. "I'm fine, really, but maybe you should drive."

"Ya think?"

Turtlezilla had remained on the bank longer than normal, the blistering sun well-nigh baking him into turtle soup. Warmed beyond comfy even with night approaching, he needed to slip back into the lake to cool off, maybe search for a snack. But he was too afraid to reenter the water.

CHAPTER THREE:
OUTBACK & THE WALKER

The conversation enroute to Outback Steakhouse in St. Augustine dominated what Pete had or hadn't seen emerge from the lake in The Refuge. He described what he thought he saw as a head only, more or less the size of a Volkswagen Beetle. Lisa countered that her father should have guzzled less alcohol and shouldn't guzzle a drop more.

Outback was packed; the only table available was a four-person booth in the first-come-first-serve bar section. The debate continued inside the restaurant.

Lisa had ordered the Victoria's Filet Mignon, bloody rare, with a loaded baked potato. Pete had ordered his usual, a Ribeye, well-done, more or less burnt, with a loaded baked potato. He'd threatened to disown Lisa for eating steak bloody rare, but her reply was always the same: 'Good luck with that.'

As they awaited their meal, Lisa sipped a J Lohr Estates Seven Oaks Cabernet Sauvignon while her father knocked back a tall Foster's with a thick coat of salt ringing the rim.

"Dad," Lisa said. "That's too much salt."

Pete replied, "That's an improvement. I thought you'd say that I've had too much beer."

Lisa retorted, "Well, that, too."

Pete changed the subject. "Listen, Kido, I'm still concerned with what I saw earlier this evening. I've told you over and over again that it wasn't normal, and it was huge. I just don't know what it was."

Lisa countered, "And I've said over and over, big fish, dad."

"No," Pete argued. "I think I saw its eyes, and I'm pretty sure I saw a curved nose."

"A curved nose," Lisa repeated indifferently. "The Proboscis Monkey has a curved nose. Maybe a monster monkey with a curved nose is swimming around in the lake."

"Yeah, real funny," Pete replied mockingly. "I'd like to think it was a turtle, but turtles don't grow that big."

A man sitting alone at the bar half-turned his head to look at Pete and his daughter upon hearing the word 'turtle.' A small man with scruffy, balding hair and a full beard with a piece of food or facsimile embedded in beard hair at the right corner of his mouth. Although the night weather was hot and sticky, he wore a long-sleeved yellow and white checkered shirt in need of washing. His khaki slacks were baggy and in need of washing. A pair of soiled white sneakers on his feet needed washing, and his clothes wafted a musky scent, but no body odor could be detected.

Pete continued, "I mean, it looked like a turtle, but with my one and only daughter doubting me, there's no hope...." Pete stopped talking as a shaggy, balding, short man stopped in front of their booth. He looked like the homeless man that he was. Pete said, "Can I help you, sir?"

The man spoke with short pauses between words. At first, Pete and Lisa both thought the man was joshing, trying to mimic Tom Hanks' character in the movie Forrest Gump, but he spoke his short-paused words with a flawless Midwestern accent. "Did... you... see... the... turtle?" he asked Pete.

Speechless for a bit, Pete finally replied, "Uh, well, sir, I saw something today, but I'm not sure what it was."

"I... seen... it," he stated.

The waitress arrived with their meal. A cute coed attending Flagler College on a lacrosse scholarship, she spoke to the homeless man. "Hey, Walker. Did you have your usual steak dinner tonight?"

"I... did," he replied. "It... was... good," then looked back at Pete. "Ain't... nobody... gonna... believe... you." He glanced at Lisa and said "Ain't... nobody... gonna... believe... him." Walker told the waitress, "Bye," then ambled out of Outback.

As the waitress served their meal, Pete asked, "Who or what was that?"

She replied, "Oh, that's Walker. He's a homeless man, we know that, but everything else is based on rumors or half-truths."

Lisa asked, "Like what?"

The waitress replied, "Well, the sheriff deputies say his real name is Bill or Bob or something like that, with the last name of Brown, but everybody calls him The Walker, or in person, Walker. He putt-putts around town on a secondhand motor scooter, a Tahoe or Tao, or something like that, but he never travels more than a few miles, maybe down to Ponte Vedra or occasionally to Daytona. He gets up at dawn and putt-putts to wherever he wants to go, gets off his scooter, and walks. He'll walk around four or five blocks all day long, and sometimes he'll walk for miles before returning to his little scooter at sunset to go home.

"Walker's out later than usual tonight. Anyway, he gets welfare, or something like that, and makes fifty bucks or so from begging on street corners. He probably stole the motor scooter. When he gets his welfare check or whatever, he'll fritter away a few bucks on a steak dinner at Outback or a lunch at the Culver's hamburger joint.

"The poor guy is mental, and he has the papers to prove it, or something like that."

Pete suggested, "He said he's seen a giant turtle."

The waitress countered, "He's probably seen Big Foot, too."

Pete asked, "He lives in St. Augustine?"

"No," she replied. "The cops say he lived in cardboard boxes for a long time, but he recently built a dwelling of some sort out of pallet boards, about the size of a minivan. Sadly, they found out where Walker's new dwelling is, and they'll have to evict him from his home soon. Poor guy. He's always getting evicted."

Pete asked, "So, where is this pallet-board dwelling?"

The waitress replied, "In a small township a few miles east of here, New St. Francisco or New St. France, or something like that."

Pete said, "New St. Francis?"

She replied, "Yeah, that's it. Poor guy. He tells people he has a house on lakefront property. Can you believe that?"

Pete looked at his daughter and raised his arms as if giving praise, tilted his head slightly to one side, and shrugged his shoulders as if saying, 'I told you so.'

Lisa retained her doubtful opinion. "Dad," she retorted in a snooty tone. "The guy is nutty as a fruitcake."

Pete replied, "I like fruitcakes."

CHAPTER 4

Bebi Barnes lived next door to Pete Colucci. Pete deemed her a 'hottie', with the face of a model, a sex bomb body, creamy smooth skin, curly black hair, a seemingly perpetual tan, and the athletic legs of a goddess. He found excuses to work in the yard when Bebi mowed her grass with a push lawn mower, taking quick peeks at her legs, those legs, flawless legs, made even more attractive by a pair of loose-fitting purplish shorts baggy enough to expose a hint of tight hips.

Her whitish tennis shoes were heavily grass stained. She habitually wore colorful body-hugging T-shirts to cover her upper torso, but the Florida heat made her sweat, sweat that stuck to the fabric like glue, her modest but perky breasts perfectly delineated with taut nipples poking at Pete as if pointing out their age disparity.

He was old enough to be her daddy, but Pete continually dreamt the impossible dream since the Sunshine State was inundated with millionaire male retirees and widowers, the root cause of eager young females pursuing a promising sugar daddy. Their pursuit was epidemic.

Pete wasn't a millionaire, but he envisaged 'young things' like his neighbor, he fantasized often, picturing Bebi Barnes naked as a Jaybird in his garden bath but had enough sense to know there wasn't that much Viagra in Florida, nor did he have faith in his daughter's offshoot product 'Stay Straight'. Advertised as capable of maintaining a four-hour erection, Pete assumed he'd be dead of a heart attack after fifteen minutes.

So, he gawked, dreamt, and wished he was younger. He did not like being old, nor did he like Bebi Barnes' boyfriend.

Pete didn't even know the guy's name and didn't care to, but he knew the bum was a wannabe gigolo. The young man never worked. His customary excuse was 'no jobs available' in a job market pleading for workers. He relied on Bebi to keep them housed and fed with her home cleaning business, or at least that's what he thought she did for a living, but he didn't care how Bebi made money, within the law, outside of the law, or prostituting her body, he didn't want to work.

The bum looked like the bum he was with greasy, long unkempt hair, a scruffy beard, dirty blue jeans, and only one T-shirt that he never washed. Bebi kept her modular home spotless and uncluttered; her backyard resembled a multicolored British rose garden. She fed the ducks often. Her bum boyfriend fed himself and drank beer.

Bebi once told Pete that she was planning to kick out the bum's worthless butt but that was four months ago, and the bum was still bumming.

Bebi loved nature and animals, a country girl with a soft heart. The bum hated nature and hated animals. He disliked Linda's dog; a rescued mutt named Dusty. They argued over Dusty constantly. The bum saw Dusty as a money pit nuisance: dog food, expensive veterinarians, constantly letting the dog in and out to pee or take a dump and persistently argued with Bebi to do the 'humane' thing by putting the dog down.

She advised the bum she'd rather put him down and made it crystal clear that if he ever mistreated Dusty, she'd slice off his family jewels with a dull knife while he slept. He never hurt Dusty, but the bum never fed the dog nor filled its water bowl and paid no attention to the mutt.

When the sun went down, lake life picked up with the noises of nature; big bullfrogs bellowing for mates, crickets chirping with their back legs, fish splashing the surface for a meal or to avoid becoming a meal, the hoots of seven species of owls, especially the Saw-whet Owl with its distinct call that sounds like a blade being sharpened with a whetstone, thus its name, Saw-whet Owl. Fenced-in dogs barked messages to other fenced-in dogs, armadillos and opossums scampered about devouring vermin that humans hate, and feral cats roamed the shore looking for something to kill, either to eat or for the sheer amusement of killing.

Bebi loved it all; the bum hated it all, but he agreed on occasion to sit by the lake with Bebi at night if he was in the mood to bellow like a bullfrog with sweet words of seduction. Bebi's acceptance over the past few months had slowly been fading into chastity.

Bebi's backyard was enclosed with the same fencing as Pete's, white panels with a chain link fence across the back and a gate for access. Pete Colucci was inside his home utilizing research engines on the internet trying to figure out what he had seen in the lake that evening. His daughter was in bed texting. As the clock moved towards midnight, Bebi and the bum, along with Dusty, walked across her backyard to the gate.

She told Dusty, "Stay here, Dusty." The dog sat obediently. He was well trained but occasionally darted out the gate with Bebi in hot pursuit. Bebi closed the gate while instructing the bum, "We're sitting on the tree stump." The old decaying stump was near the waterline, about ten yards past the last panel on the white paneled fencing. Bebi and the bum were knocking back cold beers.

"Whatever," the bum retorted, not caring where they sat, what they saw, or what they heard. The night was black as coal; no stars, no moon, but plenty of wildlife being wild. The bum nit-picked, "It's too damn hot out here, and I can't see shit!" Nor could he see what was lurking next to the last white fence panel looking for an easy meal in the undeveloped lot beside Bebi's home, its eyes following what appeared to be two large worms.

Bebi didn't care if her bum boyfriend was hot and cared even less that he couldn't see. She simply replied, "Shut up," while taking a seat on the stump before sipping more beer.

"This midnight nature bullshit sucks," he grumbled. He'd been drinking most of the evening and into the night, another reason Bebi's mood bordered on a heated argument. She'd brought home a twelve-pack of Miller High Life; she was on her second; the bum was on his tenth. "We're outa beer," he grumbled, his way of hinting that Bebi needed to find a convenience store in the middle of the night to purchase another twelve-pack.

"Jump in your truck and go buy some," she boringly suggested.

"I can't do that, and you know it, Bebi," he slurred, burping twice. "One more D.U.I. and I'll serve time."

"Then walk," she suggested, smiling, sipping more beer.

The bum didn't reply as he chug-a-lugged the last drop of beer. A blackness suddenly covered his being. It was quick, the bum too drunk to react, too drunk to realize that in a microsecond his life had ended in the mouth of a five-ton snapping turtle. He was swallowed whole, and immediately.

Dusty started barking ferociously while backing away from the gate. The barking was replaced by pitiful whines, then a howl. Bebi turned her head. She could barely see Dusty continuing his frightened retreat. "What's the matter, boy?" she asked.

Bebi wasn't drunk, which was not in her favor. She sensed a murkiness enveloping her body, like a leathery blanket, and realized a horror of some sort had engulfed her. She started to scream but a loud snap cut her body in half below the beltline before she could mutter a word. What pain she may have felt was short-lived. Those legs, those stunning muscular legs, now nothing but bloody stumps leaning against a tree stump was all that remained of Pete Colucci's 'hottie' next-door neighbor.

The huge turtle quickly swallowed her upper torso, defecated, accepted the fetid taste of what it thought might be two large worms, then leisurely slid back into the water. Except for the large worms, hunting prey in this small lake wasn't worth its energy. It dove to the bottom and reentered the limestone cavern leading to its normal domicile, an enormous, isolated swamp adjacent to The Refuge.

Larger, wider caverns below the swamp's surface gave the giant turtle access to far better sources of food in and around isolated marshlands: deer, wild boars, crocodiles, baby bears, alligators, plump manatees, any living creature big enough to make a meal, even a random big worm.

Nevertheless, the cavern leading to the smaller lake was wide enough for two yellow school buses to run its length side by side without scrapping off a shaving of yellow paint. The big turtle's carapace scrapped the limestone infrequently, but the varying widths normally made for an easy voyage, wide enough in several places for it to turn around when necessary.

Instinct would keep the turtle from reentering the smaller lake since the big caverns in the marshland offered access to better water sources. One of the caverns snaked for ten miles to the St. Johns River which offered access to shallow water opposite the Naval Air Station Jacksonville. Rarely used, the turtle didn't like the wide river due to motorized activity which occasionally cut into its carapace, and it was circumspect of a whirling beast that dropped worms into the water. Worms in shallow water offered a quick meal, but the whirling beast gave the enormous turtle pause to scavenge the murky 30-foot depths. The Navy Seals practicing airdrops from a Sikorsky SH-60 chopper never knew how lucky they were.

Dusty sprinted frantically back to the only real home he'd ever known, Bebi's modular home, but found the sliding glass door shut. He desperately pawed at the glass and whined for human help that wasn't there, then quickly darted under the shed held up by concrete blocks. He shook uncontrollably and whined for most of the night, but at long last drifted off to jittery sleep just before dawn. Dusty knew his master was gone.

CHAPTER 5

Pete Colucci awoke with a hangover at 6:00 a.m. Too many cold Foster's in a mug ringed with salt at Outback after an evening guzzling down rum and pepper destroyed too many brain cells for Pete to expect a painless morning. His daughter was leaving for Atlanta, but Pete planned to hit the sack again after she left.

Packed and ready to boogie on down the road, Lisa walked out of her bedroom perky as a puppy. Seeing her dad's condition, she couldn't resist the temptation. "You look like the southern end of a northern-bound jackass, Dad."

"Feel like it, too," he replied. "Coffee's ready."

"Great. It's nice this morning. I checked my iPhone and there is no rain predicted, so I guess the Jacksonville weather heifer is on drugs or something. I'm going to have coffee out by the lake before I leave. Do we have any flavored creamer left?"

"Yeah, in the frig," Pete said, rubbing his temples. "Make me a cup, will ya?"

"Sure."

"Did you hear Dusty barking last night?"

"Yeah," Lisa said. "He sounded pitiful." She poured two cups of coffee, added a stream of caramel creamer, stirred it a bit, and then asked her dad, "Ya want a little Captain Morgan in it?"

"Hell, no," Pete responded quickly. "Wonder what was wrong with Dusty?"

"I've never heard him bark like that before, he sounded weird," Lisa responded, handing her father a cup of hot Joe. "You want to join me by the lake before I leave?"

"Sure, but I gotta pee first. I'll meet you out there. And take the dogs with you."

"Okey-doke." Lisa walked through the sunroom accompanied by the three dogs. She opened the sunroom door. The dogs almost knocked her down scrambling out the door, either to pee, poot, chase a lizard up a tree, or any duck foolish enough to land in the backyard.

"That's okay, guys!" Lisa screamed. "I didn't need that leg anyway!" Hank, the Boston Terrier, peed, while Cloe, the mutt, sniffed the grass for a place to poot. Lily, the Chihuahua, with her remarkable sense of smell and radar ears, sprinted straight for the corner of the yard nearest Bebi Barnes' property. Stopping by the chain-linked fence, her ears shot straight up as she began barking her shrill bark. As Lisa approached the fence, she told the Chihuahua, "Chill out, Lily, it's too early for that." Lily ignored her command.

As Lily continued her shrill bark, curiosity got the best of Lisa. She walked up beside Lily, tilted her head a bit as she glanced over the chain-linked fence, said, "What'cha barking at, girl?" and took a sip of coffee. Something near the tree stump was covered with flies; a cloud of flies swarmed above, a rat and three small mice feasted, and a raccoon gnawed feverishly. Turtles had joined the banquet as had Turtlezilla, but most of the carrion was covered with dozens of Carrion Beetles so thick the carcass appeared to be black. "*What the hell?*" Lisa asked herself.

Shadows circled the area. Lisa looked up. Dozens of Floridian Turkey Vultures and Black Vultures orbited above. "That's not good," Lisa said, concerned that the meal was a neighborhood dog or cat, or more likely a deceased Muscovy duck.

As Lisa's eyes refocused on the tree stump, she realized there were two distinct pieces of carrion. Lily continued barking; Hank and Cloe joined the canine chorale; the howling and woofing hurt Lisa's ears. "Shut up, guys!" Lisa yelled but couldn't take her eyes off the frenzied activity around the tree stump. "Stay here," she commanded, then opened the gate. Hank and Cloe tried to follow. "Stay back, stay back!" Lisa screamed, play-kicking the dogs as she shut the gate.

Almost too afraid to approach the gorging, Lisa took a few steps as if walking on shattered glass. The two-piece brunch came into focus; Lisa stopped dead in her tracks. 'Oh, my God!' she screamed, dropping her coffee cup. Whatever grub remained in her stomach from Outback began its journey upward.

Her dad had just walked out, sipping coffee, temples pounding from his nasty hangover. The dogs' non-stop barking added to his morning agony. He noticed vultures circling above. "I ain't dead yet, you sonsabitches," Pete mumbled.

Lisa had panicked, shock setting in, her stomach in convulsions. "HELP! SOMEBODY HELP! OH, GOD... HELP, HELP!"

Thinking his daughter was in peril, Pete dropped his hot cup of coffee and sprinted for the fence. "LISA, LISA?" he screamed. The dogs were in a dangerous pack mode, snarling, growling, howling, their primitive genes kicking in. Pete forced the dogs aside as he opened the gate. The Chihuahua nipped his ankle, Cloe and Hank jammed the gate opening but Pete managed to shove them back with his foot. He quickly shut and locked the gate then ran to his daughter.

"LISA?" he said, softly touching her shoulder. She remained bent over, hurling up whatever was left in her stomach, the creatures behind her scattering, except for the flies and Carrion Beetles. Lisa could only point toward the tree stump.

Pete eyeballed what was left of Bebi Barnes' legs, trivial meat and exposed bone, the whitish grass-stained tennis shoes still on her feet. "Oh, God bless," he said, almost whispering as if offering condolence. A throbbing headache, rumbling stomach, barking and howling dogs, his neighbor's masticated legs, those perfect muscular legs, now an enjoyable feast for creatures big and small, all took their toll on Pete. He bent over to join Lisa in a father-daughter duet jettisoning their meals from Outback.

The stench wafting from a five-pound pile of turtle feces added to their misery.

CHAPTER 6

Chief of Police Roosevelt Jefferson was a no-nonsense type of cop. His two deputies towed a thin line, corruption was non-existent, and they respected their boss as much as they feared him. A sizable man, Chief Jefferson stood at 6'4" and tipped the scales at a brawny 260 pounds. His football scholarship to Florida State University fell by the wayside after a career-ending knee injury, hence his career in law enforcement.

He paid his dues for 30 years until elected as New St. Francis' first African American Chief of Police. He ruled the roost from a decrepit four-cell brick police station on the northern edge of the small town. Residents respectfully called him 'Chief', not Chief Jefferson, just 'Chief', he liked it and considered the moniker as an affable reference to the Florida State Seminole he used to be, and to a football career that could have been.

Behind the back comments comparing Jefferson to Sheriff Andy Taylor of Mayberry were commonplace, as were references to one of his deputies as Barney Fife and the second deputy as 'Andy's son' since his mother had named the unfortunate child Opie after Andy Taylor's offspring in the hit TV series.

Rumor had it that his last name, Jefferson, derived from mixed descendants of President Thomas Jefferson and his black slave mistress, Sally Hemings. Chief Jefferson's light caramel skin suggested a hint of truth to the rumor, but he never confirmed nor denied his ancestry. His first name, Roosevelt, paid tribute to his mother's presidential idol, Franklin Delano Roosevelt. During his childhood, she occasionally 'suggested' that her son may have Presidential blood flowing through his veins, but she never confirmed nor denied it.

The rock of the family, his mom earned a living as a domestic and raised her six kids as best she could, which meant weekly attendance at the Lily of the Valley Baptist Church. His father came and went as the man saw fit. He spent little time with his wife and even less time with his six kids.

Dark sunglasses veiled Chief Jefferson's eyes when he ventured outside, not so much to protect them from the sun's damaging rays but to make it difficult for friends and criminals alike to get a 'read' on his thoughts. Jefferson cut a handsome persona in the tan and black-striped uniform of the New St. Francis Police Department, but no cop in the state of Florida could outshine his shoes. He carried a Glock; fired once in self-defense; a 17-year-old young man took the bullet; Jefferson lived with the teenager's death every day.

Over thirty years in law enforcement hadn't prepared Jefferson for the human dismemberment around the dead tree stump in The Refuge modular home community, the cause of which he now had the responsibility of solving. His two deputies stood back from the leg bones and leftover meat while the county coroner inspected the carrion.

Two deputies, that was it, in a town of 2,000 residents in a state with a normal ratio of 2.2 officers per 1,000 residents. The lack of serious crime in New St. Francis kept the police budget far below the ratio, kept Chief Jefferson understaffed, and kept the Chief and his two deputies patrolling around town in three used police vehicles bought at auction, old Fords, underpowered, and poorly maintained.

The deputies never complained to Chief Jefferson about the passé patrol cars but habitually told hunting and fishing buddies their patrol cars were so underpowered they couldn't pull a greased string out of a turkey's ass.

Chief Jefferson stood with his hands on his hips watching the coroner do his thing from a distance, a short three steps from Pete Colucci's fence gate, awaiting his arrival. The fence gate opened; Pete Colucci approached the officer.

Pete said, "Officer, you wanted to see me?"

"Yes, sir," Jefferson responded, offering his hand for a shake. The men shook hands, then broke the shake. "Mister Colucci, I'm Chief of Police Roosevelt Jefferson, you can call me Chief. I understand that you and your daughter were first on the scene of this, this tragedy?"

"My daughter was first, Chief," Pete corrected. "I ran out here after I heard her screaming."

"Is your daughter okay, Mister Colucci?"

"She's shook-up and still sick to her stomach, but she's in bed resting, and texting, I reckon. My daughter spends most of her life texting." A strong stench hit Pete's nostrils. "There's that smell again. What the hell is that?"

"A big pile of shit," the Chief replied. "Pounds of it. We took a sample to send out for analysis. I hope it doesn't identify the stuff as coming from a Florida Panther. We'd have to hunt it down and kill it if we could ever get permission to do so since it's an endangered species."

"Damn," Pete moaned as the stench once again hit his nostrils. "Man, that burns my eyes and nose. Whew! If that stuff came out of a panther, it's a damn big panther."

Chief Jefferson had more important priorities than speculating on what type of creature dropped the five-pound pile of feces. "You're a Vietnam veteran, right?"

"How'd you know that?"

"Your Vietnam veterans license plate."

"Oh."

The Chief shifted his weight, then continued, "You were born and raised in Memphis, Tennessee. You served in Vietnam for almost three years, Air Force Intelligence, I believe. You made it home and then finished college. After which, you accepted a transportation management position at Roadway Express and retired after 30 years of employment. Now you're a journalist, author, host a radio talk show once a week, and warm a chair in the St. Augustine Poker Room almost daily. How am I doing so far?"

Dumbfounded, Pete responded, "How'd you know all that?"

"Over thirty years of know-how."

"Fine," Pete said, shrugging his shoulders. "What can I do for you, Chief?"

"You disseminated Intelligence, so you know how to evaluate, and I assume you saw much worse in Vietnam. I need a level-headed idea of what may have happened here."

Pete grasped the officer's little trap. Jefferson didn't need his participation in the investigation and Pete didn't appreciate the lawman's condescending method. He said, "Chief, I appreciate your respectful approach, but I'll be glad to account for my time last night."

A bit embarrassed and outwitted, Chief Jefferson said as much. "My bad, Mister Colucci. You've been very insightful, and you have my apology."

"No problem, Chief."

Shifting his bulky weight off his bad knee, Chief Jefferson asked, "So, where were you?"

"My daughter and I went to Outback around eight last night and left there about ten or so. My receipts can verify all that. We came home and my daughter went to bed, either sleeping or texting. I made myself a bedtime toddy, did some research on the internet, and went to bed around two this morning. I got up around six to see my daughter off to Atlanta, she went out by the lake with a cup of coffee; I heard her scream, and that's about it."

The officer was covering his investigative bases, nothing more. Besides, he already had a suspect. "What do you know about Miss Barnes's boyfriend?"

Pete's reply was short and to the point. "He's a bum."

A humorous grunt emerged from the officer. "We found some of his mail inside the house. His name is Jeffery Joe Johnson, a local boy born…."

Pete interrupted, "That's a good Irish name."

The lawman lowered his head to peer over his sunglasses, his voice raised an octave. "Like yours, Mister Colucci? I presume your Italian ancestors came over on a boat from the Boot of Ireland?"

Pete cleared his throat before meekly replying, "Sorry, please continue."

"Right," Chief Jefferson said sharply, more of a warning than a response. "As I was saying, he's a local boy, born and raised in New St. Francis, a record a mile long, but something just ain't right. As you said, he's a bum. He gets fired from jobs then applies for unemployment and lives on the unemployment for as long as he can while leeching off women until they kick out his lazy ass, but he's nothing but a punk.

"All his offensives are petty stuff, shoplifting or breaking into a fishing shack for rods and reels, public drunkenness, a couple of D.U.I.'s, and stuff like that. But Jeffery Joe doesn't have the balls to do something like this." Jefferson nodded at the remains.

Pete speculated, "Do you think he's on the run?"

Smacking his lips, frowning, hesitating for a few seconds while scratching the back of his head, the lawman then replied, "Well, just in case he and parts of the girl are in the lake, I'm sending down two divers from the St. Augustine Sheriff's Department tomorrow afternoon when they return from Daytona. A kid fell off a speedboat, a state senator's kid; and his body hasn't been recovered yet, so every diving resource in the area is down at Daytona today. Anyway, if Jeffery Joe is on the run, then he's running on his feet because his old truck is still in the driveway. So is her Honda."

"That is weird," Pete commented. He thought about what he may or may not have seen the day before, then asked, "Is it possible something in the lake killed her, maybe him, too?"

A panther. A bear. A large wild animal. Any ground-pounding predator might be an option, but a lake creature? "Like what?" Jefferson asked Pete.

"I don't know, maybe a big alligator? I'm not a native Floridian so I'm not familiar with the large predators in this state."

Skeptical, if not amused, the Chief replied, "It's doubtful a big gator is down there. It would have been spotted long ago by your neighbors." But any possibility could not be ruled out. "I'll have the divers look around for any abnormal lake life, but I'm fairly certain we're looking for a land beast or human beast."

Pete remembered Dusty, Bebi's mutt. "She has a dog."

"Yeah, he's in the house hiding in the laundry room. We found him under the shed, shaking like a leaf, half scared to death. He probably saw what happened last night… I wish that dog could talk."

A soft heart for animals his entire life, Pete asked, "What will happen to him?"

Chief Roosevelt Jefferson was a dog owner and dog lover, three mutts and two retired police dogs kept his yard well-fertilized. The sadness was reflected in his voice. "He'll have to go to the St. Augustine Animal Control people."

Pete detected the despondency in the lawman's voice. "Are they no-kill?"

Jefferson was painfully honest. "They try to be, but as always, space is limited. The save rate for dogs is around ninety-three percent, but a cat's save rate is about thirty-one percent unless they're kittens. I avoid the place; I have too many dogs already. One more dog brought home will cost me a divorce."

Pete knew his neighbor's dog was a last-minute rescue, enjoyed its home, had no mean streaks, and got along with other dogs. Pete offered, "Sir, I'll foster Dusty until we can find him a new home."

Chief Jefferson was genuinely thankful. "That's compassionate of you, Mister Colucci, thank you."

"I like dogs, Chief."

Jefferson admitted, "Me, too, Mister Colucci, I got five of them, I like dogs," then nodded toward Linda Barnes' home. "But that poor dog in there sure didn't like something it saw last night."

* * * * *

Pete walked across his yard to the sunroom's back door, all the while picturing what Bebi Barnes used to look like and what was left of her to look at now. He felt sickness and sympathy, and the Chief was right;

Pete had seen a lot worse in Vietnam, yet the Chief's reference to Pete's service brought back graphic memories he'd tried to suppress for years. Enough experience in combat can dull the horror of seeing the dead, the dying, the wounded, the vaporized, the dismembered, but not chewed up remains of the woman next door.

Whatever happened to Bebi Barnes, whatever killed her, human or beast, didn't show any pity, no hesitation; Pete could only hope her death had been a quick one.

He re-entered his house, poured straight Captain Morgan into a purple Solo cup, downed half of it, and then quietly ambled to the open door to Lisa's bedroom. He peaked inside. She lay curled up in a fetal position, apparently sleeping; all three dogs piled up on her bed. Pete started to back away, not wanting to wake her.

"Dad," Lisa said, sitting up on the bed. A little startled, Pete said, "Dang, you scared me, Kido. Thought you were asleep."

"I wish I could sleep," she replied. "What happened out there, Dad?"

"I don't know," he answered truthfully. "And I don't think the police have a clue, except for a pile of manure."

"Yeah, I remember that horrible smell, but how can it be part of what happened to Bebi."

"I don't know, I just don't know. Listen, Kido, it's been a hell of a morning. Rest up and wait until tomorrow to get on the road. Can we agree on that?"

"Agreed," Lisa said, blinking her eyes as if calculating her next question. "What about that 'thing' you saw yesterday?"

Pete had already thought of the 'thing' he may or may not have seen possibly poking its head up in the lake or perhaps not, and if what he saw or didn't see was the head of a big creature or a piece of wood or an old rowboat, what's dangerous about it or not dangerous? Rationalization deserted his logic. He told his daughter, "I didn't tell the police about it."

"And why not?" Lisa drilled.

"Well, for one thing, I didn't want to sound like a raving lunatic, plus I'm not sure I saw anything, it could have been the booze or the heat… hell, my eyesight, I don't know, Kido, I can't prove anything."

"I wish we could. I think the answer may be at the bottom of the lake."

Interesting comment, Pete thought, then asked his daughter for clarification. "Why do you think that?"

"I've been Googling. One of the deepest lakes in Florida is Big Lake, about ninety feet deep, just south of Lake Okeechobee in the Big Cypress National Preserve. It's just a large sinkhole."

"Okay," Pete said, impressed if not gratified with his offspring's inquisitiveness. "What's your point?"

"The word "ONE" of the deepest lakes, that's what bothers me. There are other secluded lakes, basically sinkholes, that could be deeper that haven't been discovered or explored yet. This state is one big sinkhole, unstable ground, with underground rivers running through the porous limestone. Our backyard may be a beach one day, or maybe a scuba-diving destination, especially since a lot of Florida's natural springs are drying up."

"Do what?" Pete responded.

"Yeah," Lisa said. "The natural springs are used for irrigation and drinking water. The freshwater is getting lower and lower while the seawater beneath seeps up higher and higher. It's sad, many of Florida's former freshwater springs have become stagnated and the tourist traps surrounding them have already closed their doors."

Pete commented, "I had no idea."

Lisa continued, "Most people don't. It's not the type of subject people care about. Anyway, sinkholes are all over America, people vacation to them and swim in them, one big sinkhole in Texas has claimed the lives of seven divers, so far. Sinkholes can be picturesque, but equally dangerous." Lisa paused as if to finalize her theory.

"And?" Pete egged her on.

"That lake out there. We were told it's natural and deep, but we weren't told how deep. Maybe they don't know, maybe it's an old sinkhole a hundred feet or so deep. Maybe big caverns of limestone are down there, maybe it's fed by a natural spring or underground river…" She shrugged her shoulder. "Hell, I don't know, but something may be down there that's… I don't know," Lisa tilted her head. "That's big enough to kill a human?"

"Good thought, and good research, Kido," Pete said. Could his daughter be correct? Could an enormous old alligator or other species big enough to kill and consume a human be lurking in the depths of a Florida lake? Were they both nuts for thinking so? And would Chief Jefferson believe such a madcap tale? If the 'thing' never resurfaced; if he never saw it again, if nobody else ever spotted the 'thing', if it had died, drowned; walked or crawled away into obscurity, or killed and eaten by a larger and stronger predator, then his 'proof' would disappear along with anyone thinking he was mentally sound. But maybe there was a way. Pete asked his daughter, "Kido, did I ever tell you about the times I went scuba diving in Heber Springs, Arkansas?"

CHAPTER 7

Lisa tossed an overnight bag into the back seat of her VW Jetta and slid into the driver's seat, feigning anger but was worried sick for her stubborn father standing next to the open driver's door. "Okay, I'm leaving for Atlanta; I have no choice, I have to get back to protect my business. You're more hardheaded than I am, which means I'm probably wasting my breath, but *don't you dare* scuba dive in that lake! We have no idea what's out there and I love you as a whole person, not a pair of bloody leg stumps! And you're too old to scuba dive! You haven't had a tank on your back since…."

Pete interrupted his daughter's rant. "Uh, Kido, didn't we have this same conversation last night?"

"Yeah!" she responded, tetchily. "And you had an asinine smirk on your face then and you have the same asinine smirk on your face now! You said you wouldn't go in the lake, but I trust you less than I do Congress!"

Pete grinned. "Damn, Kido, that's a real low blow."

"Dad, I'm serious!" she retorted, a bit calmer, but her eyes still flinging poisoned darts. "Promise me you won't do it."

Pete lowered his head, his eyes locked into his favorite Michael Corleone cold stare. Lisa recognized the look, her father's way of saying *'back off'* that bordered on an expected disciplinary outburst of independence. Pete's attitude had served him well throughout his life, a mindset honed by peace and war, love and hate, and trust destroyed by deceit. Pete didn't dislike his fellow man; he just didn't have faith in their ability to have faith in him.

The only real brotherhood he'd known was in Vietnam, the faith in the man next to him and the realization that war produces the worst in man but also the best in man. Civilized life, a watchword Pete considered an oxymoron, encompassed more booby traps than the Viet Cong ever laid.

Sociable, but cautious; compassionate, but suspicious; loving, but selective in his affection and friendships, many of his associates considered Pete cold when he was only being careful. He seldom asked for or took advice from anyone; his self-defense apparatus warned him against unsolicited counsel; Pete liked to figure out things by himself, found the authenticity by himself, and in this case, perhaps discover the source by himself.

Lisa gave up. "Fine, go ahead, see if I care, end up fish food in rubber flippers." But she did care. "Okay, give me a goodbye hug." Pete bent over for a loving hug. Lisa broke the hug and asked her father. "Just be careful, is that too much to ask?"

"No, it's not," Pete replied. "And I'll be careful. Be sure to text or call me when you arrive in Atlanta. And drive safe, you hear me, Kido?"

"I will," she said, pushing the start button. The Jetta hummed to a good start. Lisa gunned it twice before looking back up at her father. "See ya in a few weeks, Dad, okay?"

Pete knew the 'okay?' really meant 'don't be foolish, don't take chances, and 'I love you.'

"You bet'cha, Kido," he said. "Don't forget to text me."

"I will." She backed out into the street, waved, and was gone.

"Now," Pete said to himself. "Where in this thriving metropolis can a guy rent scuba equipment without Rebel flags painted on the tank?"

* * * * *

A hot, humid, sticky afternoon, but not as mentally hot as Chief Jefferson. He was in no mood for what he considered foolish and unprofessional behavior by the two scuba divers on loan from the St. Johns County Sheriff's Department. The small tax base in New St. Francis equated to a small police department, which created a red-headed stepchild syndrome for Jefferson and his two deputies when resources lacked the necessary law enforcement equipment. The smartass remarks from the two diving deputies crawled under Jefferson's skin.

"Think we'll find Godzilla," diver White asked the other.

"Could be Jaws," diver Middleton teased.

"Lake's not that big. Could be a large catfish."

"Or a Goldfish."

Jefferson blew his top. "I can tell ya what's NOT in the lake, you two bozos! I have what remains of a young lady's legs and her vagrant boyfriend is missing. The rest of the girl may be down there, her boyfriend may be down there, but YOU TWO ain't! Get your asses in the water or be thrown in!"

Professionalism remained intact between the affable Sheriff of St. Johns County and Chief Jefferson, but below the surface of respectability lurked a sense of superiority from the deputies of St Johns County versus the unjustified Barney Fife reputation of the two New St. Francis deputies and Chief Jefferson. The two scuba divers did nothing other than stare at Chief Jefferson as if evaluating a maniac in a police uniform.

Chief Jefferson was livid. "Put on those frog-eyes and get your asses in the water.... NOW!"

Angering Roosevelt Jefferson was more dangerous than calling mafia families a pack of greaseballs in a newspaper featuring an expose on organized crime. His reputation as 'tough' had not diminished with age; if anything, he was tougher now than as a young man, but lately, his short fuse was shorter than normal, a quick explosion of fury an almost daily occurrence. One young recruit from Ocala had recently offended Roosevelt Jefferson in the parking lot at a law enforcement convention in Jacksonville. Jefferson bodily picked up the recruit like a bag of potatoes and lobbed him nonchalantly over his patrol car then ambled away.

Nobody said a word, but 'the word' spread like wildfire through every law enforcement agency in Florida. The two scuba divers mellowed quickly, responding in unison, "Yes, sir," and donned their diving masks. They never made it into the water.

CHAPTER 8

Distracted by Chief Jefferson's ire and threatening demeanor, knowing full well that this hulk of a man didn't bluff and cared not for any form of disrespect, the two St. Johns County scuba divers had failed to notice the water bubbles approaching their entry position at water's edge. Slipping on their diving masks while facing each other, they turned to enter the lake.

Puffed up like an irritated pufferfish, Jefferson's wrathful gaze centered on the backs of the two brazen-faced scuba divers about to enter the water. That these two deputies worked for a wealthy county and made twice the salary he did, added to the Chief's resentment, perhaps more from jealousy and less from perceived disrespect. Jefferson was first to notice the air bubbles and a blackish figure beneath the water closing in on where the deputies stood. *An alligator* was his first and only thought.

"STOP!" Jefferson yelled at the divers while reaching for his holstered Glock. Confused by the order, seeing the sheriff pull his Glock and aim between them, the two divers thought the man had lost his sanity. "Move back, QUICK!" Jefferson yelled. The divers awkwardly scrambled from the water's edge and stood beside the Chief as he took a bead on the emerging object.

All decked out in a black wetsuit and scuba gear, Pete Colucci surfaced a few feet from shore. Removing his diving mask, Pete found a welcoming committee comprised of two scuba divers and Chief Roosevelt Jefferson with a two-handed grip on a Glock aimed straight at Pete's chest. The sheriff muttered an obscenity as he lowered the Glock. An odd, baffling moment passed before Pete said, "Afternoon, Chief."

Beyond furious, Jefferson grumbled, "Jesus H. Christ," then turned his wrath on Pete with more of a damning rant than a simple question. "What the hell do you think you're doing, Colucci!"

Pete replied the obvious, "Scuba diving."

The truth upset the Chief more than a dumb reply. "Oh, is that a fact! I thought perhaps you were on your way to Red Lobster for dinner!" The Chief pointed at the long yellow police tape surrounding the tree stump and adjacent area. "That yellow police tape indicates a crime scene, or don't you ever watch crime shows on TV!"

Again, Pete replied the obvious, "I'm not inside the damn tape."

The two scuba divers took a step back, not sure what kind of response to expect from Chief Jefferson, but a token example of 'police brutality' crossed their minds. It was not unheard of for the law enforcement of New St. Francis to ignore their legal authority and bust a few hardheaded heads to restore law and order, at least by their definition of law and order. No lawsuits had ever been filed against the three officers, but their archaic form of justice contributed to an almost non-existent criminal element in New St. Francis.

Troublemakers usually know where they can initiate trouble without getting into too much trouble. New St. Francis' was not on their list of destinations. The City Council and residents never complained; they enjoyed walking the streets at night, obeyed the laws, didn't fear for their kids to play at the town's only park, and most agreed that peace and safety come at a price.

But common sense also played a vital part in the law in New St. Francis. Chief Jefferson holstered his Glock; knew his outburst had been out of line, then attempted a better approach. "Okay, Colucci," he said in his normal voice, which was stern enough. "I apologize for shouting at you, but I'd appreciate an explanation for why you went scuba diving in the lake."

"Curiosity," Pete replied. "And a hunch, maybe even a clue. I saw something yesterday evening that I can't explain. It came up from the lake for a moment then disappeared, and I think what came up was only its head. It was big, Chief, but I didn't get a good look at it."

"Did you find any remains in the lake?"

"No, but I didn't reach the bottom. As you can tell, I'm not in good enough shape for a deep dive, plus this wetsuit is too thin for a deeper dive. It was cold down there, real cold. I stopped at fifty feet, but I've never seen clearer water. I could see the bottom, about a hundred feet down. No remains that I could see."

Diver White commented, "There's no lake that deep in Florida."

Pete responded, "Well, this one is. Several of Florida's isolated lakes and sinkholes have never been fully explored, especially by scuba divers, you know that as well as I do."

Diver White didn't respond, but his hesitation to answer stirred Chief Jefferson's curiosity. "Answer the man," he instructed.

White's reply was humble. "Yeah, he's right."

Jefferson's response lacked humbleness but reeked of sarcasm. "Well, thank you, Deputy White, that's mighty white of you!" The deputy lowered his head and said not a word.

"Chief," Pete said, regaining Jefferson's attention. "There are caverns at the bottom. I could see them, but as I said, I didn't dive deep enough to explore. I don't know if they are caves or tunnels or just eroded limestone, but the mouth of one cavern is enormous."

Realizing the possibility of a clue, however remote, Jefferson instructed the divers, "You two get down there and find out if anything worthwhile is on the bottom and take a good look at those caverns." Donning their diving masks, the two deputies flopped their fins forward and then cautiously entered the lake, leaving the two men on the bank to engage in small talk until they resurfaced.

Middleton and White quickly discovered the veracity in Pete's comments. The deeper they dove, the clearer the water, more like a gigantic aquarium than a natural lake, and cold. Sunlight creates the Euphotic zone of visibility nearer the top of a lake, but the Limnetic zone near and on the bottom is normally dark and without plant life. Not this little lake. And it was deep, 110 feet according to Middleton's Scubapro wrist-mounted depth gauge, and unpleasantly cold at forty degrees according to its built-in temperature gauge. Both divers wore twin scuba tanks with a usual yellow Octopus hose hanging from their regulators for an alternate air source in case their primary tanks stopped providing life-saving oxygen.

Diver White tapped Middleton's shoulder to gain his attention and then pointed at the biggest cavern. The opening was large enough to easily drive an army tank into it, and the remarkably radiant light inside the cavern provided incredible visibility at the bottom of the lake, although visibility faded further out. The divers had never seen anything quite like it, but what was the light source? What illuminated a neighborhood lake over 100 feet below the surface? Middleton pointed towards the opening. They were going in.

Middleton entered the cavern first but stopped ten feet in and motioned for White to not enter. White stopped at the mouth of the cavern and grabbed a segment of protruding limestone with his left hand to steady his buoyancy. Middleton ran his fingers along deep scars grooved into the limestone sides of the cavern, glanced into the brightness further in, and noticed that the cavern gave way to a long tunnel progressively ascending upward. Middleton turned towards White, halfway raised his arms then shrugged his shoulders, as if baffled, which he was.

White didn't respond. He'd felt a sharp pain on his left hand and saw blood filtered into the lake water. White jerked his hand away from the protruding limestone, saw that his index finger was severely lacerated, then glanced at his partner for assistance. Middleton saw blood pooling in the water around White's left hand and immediately swam to his injured diving buddy.

Deprived of his snack, Turtlezilla moseyed away from the bright cavern.

*****

Pete and the Chief had just about run out of small

talk as both divers emerged from the water. White's blood-dripping hand was too obvious not to notice.

Jefferson asked, "What happened to you?"

White replied, "A damn snapper! The sonavabitch almost took off my finger!"

Pete asked, "How big was it?"

White replied, "Biggest one I've ever seen, big around as a hula-hoop."

Pete said, "That's Turtlezilla."

Jefferson heard it but couldn't believe it. "A what?"

"Turtlezilla," Pete repeated. "I named it Turtlezilla. He's been in the lake for God knows how long, most likely hatched here and survived here. He's a big'un."

Chief Jefferson asked, "Think his big daddy is in there?" Pete shrugged his shoulders in an evasive answer. "Middleton," the Chief said, turning his attention to the two divers. "Get White to the hospital, and I want a detailed report from both of you."

Middleton replied, "Chief, Mister Colucci was right. There's a cavern, well, it's really a tunnel down there big enough to park a locomotive inside. The limestone walls are scarred as if they were scraped by, I don't know, by something, something big. And the tunnel illuminates a bright light. Never seen anything like it."

"Told ya," Pete added.

"Very well," the Chief said as if accepting the unacceptable. "I want you two or a couple of your buddies back in the morning to explore that cavern... or cave, tunnel, whatever the hell you want to call it."

"Yes, sir," Middleton muttered, then told White. "Com'on, let's go."

As soon as the divers were out of hearing distance, Jefferson informed Pete, "I'm off duty."

Not able to decipher why the lawman wanted Pete to know his working hours, he softly replied with a question, as if seeking the reason. "Okay?"

The officer's reply was unexpected. "Ya got a drink?"

CHAPTER 9

Chief Jefferson slouched more than sat in the large chair in front of the TV. Pete sat on the couch with his two big dogs; the Chihuahua had crawled under her blankie after several attempts to nip the lawman's ankles. Bebi's dog, Dusty, was still at the veterinarian's getting checked out before being introduced to his new home. Pete nor the Chief had said a word other than the officer saying, "Thanks," when Pete handed him a solo cup filled to the brim with spiced rum and Dr. Pepper Cream Soda.

The scuba gear was in the sunroom, plainly visible to Jefferson through the inside glass door. Before taking his first sip, he commented, "I can't believe you rented scuba gear with a rebel flag painted on the tank."

Pete responded, "That was the only tank available. This town isn't exactly a diver's paradise."

"Got that right," Jefferson responded, taking his first sip. He'd never tasted rum and pepper. "What the hell kind of drink is this?"

Pete grinned, then replied, "Captain Morgan Spiced Rum mixed with Dr. Pepper Cream Soda."

"Is that a fact," Jefferson said as he took another sip. "Hummm, sort of grows on you."

"That's what my daughter said," Pete stated. "What's on your mind, Chief?"

"Well, people are nosey, so we're telling your neighbors around the lake that we're investigating a freak drowning, possibly a gator attack. I'm pretty sure that you and your daughter are the only ones to see Miss Barnes' remains. Of course, we're also asking if anyone has seen her boyfriend."

Pete knew Chief Jefferson was beating around the bush, so he repeated, "What's on your mind, Chief?"

Getting to the meat of the meeting, Jefferson looked at Pete and then asked, "How well did you know your neighbor, Bebi Barnes?"

"Every time I looked at her; I wished I was 30 years younger."

"Besides that," Jefferson said. "What do you know about her personal life?"

"She didn't choose her men too well. Speaking of which, have you found the bum yet?"

"Nope. Keep going."

"Bebi was country as corn, but clever, possibly well-educated, which baffled me about her choice in men. She came and went at strange hours with her cleaning business, with no regular schedule to my knowledge. Quite frankly, I don't know what she was doing for a living, but it wasn't a cleaning business."

Jefferson grunted like an old bull, took a big gulp of rum and pepper, licked his lips, and replied, "Interesting. Why do you think that?"

"I've shaken her hand twice, smooth hand, not a cleaning hand, well-manicured nails, her working clothes are never soiled; and I've seen the cleaning equipment she unloads from her car. The mop bucket is always clean, the mop looks brand new, and the cleaning liquid in some of the plastic bottles is always the same level. Her cleaning rags are never dirty. I didn't think anything of it the first few times, but after two years of seeing the same thing over and over… well, something just didn't jell."

Chief Jefferson stared at Pete for a moment; then asked, "Are you always that observant?"

"Just bored."

"Bored?"

"Well, in my opinion, it was too obvious, like Bebi was faking having a cleaning business." Pete sipped his rum and pepper, rethought his statement, and then said, "I could be wrong, but I don't think so."

Shifting his weight in the chair before finishing his drink, Chief Jefferson informed Pete, "Bebi was a pro, most likely the best undercover agent the Florida Bureau of Investigation ever had. A Master's Degree in Criminology, proficient in three languages, yeah, she was a country girl, but could easily be a jet setter for one assignment or a cowgirl from Texas on her

next endeavor. Her only flaw was being a bum mag-
net, but I guess that came from needing to date men
who were too ignorant to figure out what she did for
a living."

Pete was straightforward with his remark. "What
a waste; she was such a good-looking girl. So, was she
on an assignment in New St. Francis?"

"No, this was her home. She worked the entire
state, but once her duty was done, she always came
home to New Saint Francis and the life she loved.
She enjoyed wildlife, the seclusion, and especially
the quietness… she was a good girl. I'm the only one
around here who knew her real occupation."

"What a waste," Pete repeated.

Chief Jefferson stared into nothingness, seemingly lost in deep thought about something other than
Bebi Barnes' death. Pete started to interrupt Jefferson's silence, but the lawman finally mumbled, "Yes, a
waste," and then slid back into a daze.

Pete didn't know exactly what to do. The Chief of
Police of New St. Francis appeared to be in a trance,
frozen in time or perhaps in the past, with too much
rumination and not enough reality. Pete noticed that
Jefferson was losing his grip on the Solo cup, the cup
slowly tilting, the ingredients near spillage. Using the
Solo cup as an excuse to break Jefferson's concentra-
tion, Pete warned, "Chief, you're going to spill your
drink."

Jefferson slowly turned his head, his eyes glazed over, his tone softer than normal, "What?"

"Your drink! You're going to spill your drink!"

"Oh," Jefferson mumbled, gripping the cup tighter, emerging from his stupor or daydream, returning from wherever he may have been. "Yes, I… well, tell me about your buddy in the lake, this Turtlezillion."

"It's Turtlezilla."

"Whatever."

"I don't know, it's a big snapping turtle, that's all I know about him. He's not friendly, I know that. I've tried to talk to the guy several times, but he refuses to engage in conversation."

Jefferson was not in the mood for amusement. "Cute, Colucci, real cute. I've called in a herpetologist from the University of Florida."

That was a new one to Pete. "What's that, a herpes expert?"

"No, it's a specialist with amphibians and reptiles," Jefferson replied. He used the word herpetologist because it was the only one of several monikers he could pronounce for a turtle expert, including cheloniologist, chelonologist, testudinologist, or in layman's terms, a turtle expert.

Jefferson continued, "The preliminary analysis on the pile of crap we found on the bank indicated it came from a turtle, we don't know what kind, but most likely a snapping turtle. But your Turtlezilla buddy didn't dump it, he's too small. I'm thinking what you saw in the lake may be a huge snapper, perhaps a freak of nature."

Pete replied truthfully. "I was hoping I was wrong. Chief, if that 'thing' I saw is real, then we have a hell of a problem out there."

"Yeah, I know," Jefferson mumbled. "I'm starting to feel like Sheriff Brody in Jaws. But this ain't Amity Island and you ain't Quint, hell, you don't even own a boat, much less a bigger boat. Colucci, I'll tell you one thing, if that herpetologist looks like Richard Dreyfuss and his last name is Hooper, hell, I might shoot myself."

Pete burst out laughing. "Ya want another drink, Chief?"

"Yeah, I do." Then surprised Pete when he asked, "You want to help?"

That did surprise Pete. He wasn't comfortable with being asked and even more uncomfortable with the idea. "How can I help?"

"Help me figure out this thing. I trusted your neighbor, Bebi Barnes, but I don't trust the St. Augustine divers. To them, this town might as well be Mayberry. We're compared to Mayberry all the time behind my back, hell, I know that, especially with a deputy named Opie. But by God, we keep the peace. If the St. Augustine divers or deputies solve anything they'll take all the credit, but if they don't solve anything, if nothing is found and I don't solve this case, well, I'll be the laughingstock of every law enforcement agency in the state of Florida."

"I repeat," Pete stated. "How can I help?"

"Go down with the divers tomorrow morning as my… my special assistant. Yeah, that sounds good. Watch the divers, observe the cavern, and listen to the divers when they report to me. I want the truth, not a condescending speech from better-than-thou St. Augustine deputies."

Pete managed a doubtful grin. "You're nuts, you know that?"

Jefferson didn't hesitate, "I know that. I just figured you're as nutty as I am."

"Well, that is interesting," Pete said. "How did you make that assessment?"

"Easy," Jefferson replied. "A man your age in the shape you're in, thinking he's still young, scuba diving in a lake that contains possible human remains, using a tank with a rebel flag painted on the back, taking irrational risks that you don't need to take. Hell, Colucci, does that sound sane to you?"

"I'm just bored," Pete countered.

"You mentioned that once already," Jefferson said. "So, you're bored, and I think you're nuts, just like me. I need help, I need you down there tomorrow with those deputies, I need to know the truth. Think you can do it?"

"I've never been down that deep."

"Think you can do it?" Jefferson repeated.

Pete finished his drink. Considering his age, a polite refusal was in order, or any other acceptable humbug response. Pete dilly-dallied, attempted to drink from an empty cup as he envisioned the clear water, the large cavern, the bright light, what may live in or trek the limestone pathway. But he just couldn't visualize a turtle the size of a space shuttle, maybe twice the size. Lisa's words, *'And you're too old to scuba dive,'* rang as a reasonable warning and proper refutation to Chief Jefferson. *'My special assistant,'* the lawman had suggested.

Pete grunted, snickered, and rubbed what hair remained on his noggin. A hundred feet dive, far beyond his experience, especially with a solo tank with only enough oxygen for 20 minutes at that depth, probably less.

Chief Jefferson sensed a negative response on the tip of Pete's tongue, so he played his trump card. "You're taking too long to decide, so you want to do this but you're too afraid to admit it."

Pete chuckled. Curiosity outfoxed his common sense, it always did. "That's good reverse phycology, Chief. Okay, you got your special assistant."

Jefferson grinned a big satisfying grin. "Good. Now, how about that drink?"

Pete chuckled again. "You bet'cha."

CHAPTER 10

The St. Augustine Sheriff divers, Middleton and Burke, entered the water to start their slow descent into the depths of the lake behind Pete Colucci's property. Middleton's diving buddy from the day before, White, was not allowed to dive due to his injury, compliments of Turtlezilla.

A paramedic sat in one of Colucci's lawn chairs sipping on a morning coffee. Chief Jefferson had demanded a paramedic, not a less qualified EMT. He had a gut instinct the paramedic would be needed, if not caused by the snapper called Turtlezilla, then perchance by whatever lurked inside the limestone tunnel.

Jefferson was nervous, he feared the unknown, something was down there, and he didn't trust the St. Augustine divers to respond aggressively if push came to shove. They were family men, Jefferson had met their families once at a banquet, but Pete Colucci seemed eccentric enough to push, shove, and willing to engage if push then shove wasn't enough. Jefferson was wrong about the deputies, even wrong concerning Pete.

"You ready?" Jefferson asked Pete.

"Yeah, I guess so," Pete replied. "Wish I had a thicker wetsuit, it's damn cold down there."

Jefferson pointed at the dive knife sheathed on Pete's right calf. "What'cha plan to do with that?" he teased.

"In case I run into a turtle the size of a cabin cruiser," Pete shot back.

"Ya plan to kill it with a knife?" the lawman continued to tease.

"Nope," Pete responded. "If it attacks me, I plan to kill myself." Preparing to don his diving mask, Pete maundered, "I must be bat-shit crazy to do this."

Jefferson grinned. "Well, I appreciate your bat-shitiness."

"Right," Pete responded, gloomily. They didn't notice the man rounding the corner of the paneled fence.

Approaching the two men, he asked, "Excuse me, are you Chief Jefferson?"

Pete and the Chief turned their heads. The man stood at 5'8", with unruly curly brown hair, an untrimmed mustache, and ratty whiskers impersonating a beard. A distinguished nose held up thin-rimmed Granny glasses. Nike tennis shoes on his feet, frayed blue jeans, a bleached white T-shirt, and a beat-up fisherman's hat hung on his back held in place by a hat string around his neck. Notepad in hand, a pen clipped to the neck of his T-shirt; Richard Dreyfuss, Jr. crossed both their minds.

Pete asked Jefferson, "You're not going to shoot yourself, are you?"

"I might," Jefferson muttered, then asked the man, "And who might you be?"

The man stuck out his hand for a handshake. "I'm Ron Hooten, Professor of Herpetology at the University of Florida. I believe you requested my assistance."

Chief Jefferson broke the handshake. "Hooten, not Hooper?"

Hooten laughed. "I get that all the time, sir. Yeah, I sort of look like Matt Hooper in the movie but believe me, that's it. He can keep his Great Whites; I'll stick to turtles."

"So, how can you help us, Mr. Hooten?" Jefferson asked. "We are at a loss here. And call me Chief."

"Fine. I've already helped you, Chief," Hooten responded. "I examined the girl's remains, but there's not enough meat and bone left to determine what may have snapped off her legs. But I did…"

Pete couldn't help himself. "So, this was no boating accident?"

Jefferson lowered his head, rubbed his temples, and shook his head in disbelief at Pete's imprudent question. Hooten was not distracted. "No, sir, it was not a boating accident, and this isn't Jaws. That poor girl died a horrible death. And you are?"

Pete offered his hand. "Pete Colucci, Mr. Hooten,

I live in the house right behind you. Sorry for the smart-ass remark."

As Hooten broke the handshake, he replied, "Nice to meet you, Mister Colucci. Considering the situation, I guess a little humor is permissible." He scanned Pete's scuba gear. Nodding at the lake, he asked, "Are you planning to go down there, sir?"

"Yep," Pete said, nodding at the Chief. "His idea."

"Humm," Hooten hummed then returned his attention to Chief Jefferson. "Chief, as I said, whatever snapped off or cut off the girl's legs, well, I can't determine from the remains as to what happened, there's not enough remaining to do so. I did put the feces under a microscope and from that, I think I may have identified the animal it came from."

"A snapper?" Pete conjectured.

"Worse than that, Mister Colucci."

Jefferson interrupted immediately. "Worse? How can it be worse if we're dealing with some freak of Mother Nature that we think may be a snapper?"

"Sir, I'm just taking an educated guess the feces came from an Alligator snapping turtle." The blank stares from the two men indicated their ignorance of the difference. Hooten continued, "Let me explain the difference. An Alligator..."

"Wait a minute, Hooper," Jefferson interrupted, holding his right hand up as if to stop Hooten physically. He dropped his hand. "I'm no expert on..."

"It's Hooten, not Hooper," Hooten corrected.

"Whatever," Jefferson countered. "I'm no turtle expert, but I know an Alligator snapping turtle is one mean sonavabitch, is that correct?"

"Yes, sir."

"A common snapper can take off a finger, so if an Alligator…"

"No, sir, it can't."

"What?"

"There's no documented case where a common snapper took off a human finger, or a toe, or anything else. They can cause some bad injuries, but whereas they have powerful jaws they aren't as dangerous as an Alligator snapper."

"Fine," the Chief said, shifting his weight. "Tell us about this Alligator snapper and the difference."

"Yes, sir," Hooten began. "The largest common snapper caught in the wild reportedly weighed seventy-five pounds; that said and done, in 1937 an Alligator snapper was captured in Kansas that weighed approximately four hundred and three pounds."

Pete commented, "That's a damn big turtle."

Hooten replied, "Yes, sir, a damn big one. The carapace of the common snapper is rough but smooth compared to an Alligator snapper's carapace. It has three dorsal ridges on its shell which gives it a prehistoric type of appearance. We once thought only one species existed, but a second species was recently found in the Suwannee River.

"It, naturally, is called a Suwannee Alligator Snapping Turtle. On land, an Alligator snapper is dangerous and can be aggressive, but in water, they normally swim away from humans as if not wanting contact. Its jaws are very powerful, it can snap through a broom handle. So human fingers and toes don't stand a chance, on the other hand, no human deaths by an Alligator snapper have ever been recorded."

Pete asked, "Okay, so, are you saying there's a gigantic Alligator snapping turtle in this lake?"

Hooten replied, "No, sir. I'm suggesting the feces conceivably came from an unknown species of Alligator snappers, that's my educated guess. But to be sure, I have sent a sample overnight express to the I.U.C.N. for…."

Jefferson interrupted, "The who?"

Hooten replied, "The International Union for Conservation of Nature. Their S.S.C. is…"

Jefferson interrupted again, "Hooten, stop with the initials."

"Yes, sir," he agreed. "Their Special Services Committee. In my opinion, they're the best turtle experts in America. But so far as to what's in that lake…" Hooten nodded toward the water. "…I have no idea what's out there."

Jefferson suggested, "Then just maybe we have an

old Alligator snapper in the lake, possibly one that never stopped growing?"

Hooten replied, "I guess anything is possible, but it's doubtful a mature one would keep on growing. A common snapper can live a hundred years or so, but an Alligator snapper may live to 200 years or more. To be honest, we don't know their lifespan, and we may never know."

Pete asked, "Do you know anything about weird lights inside a cave or tunnel? One of the bigger tunnels down there emits a light source of some kind."

Hooten replied, "Mr. Colucci, that's most likely cyanobacteria photosynthesizing. Caves use what's called far-red light and other versions of chlorophyll to generate energy, in this case probably generating the light source you see. Your tunnel or cave is probably hollowed-out Capitan limestone containing microbes, which allow full sunlight near the opening to what's called twilight zones deeper inside a cave or cavern. I'd have to employ an irradiance meter to measure the level of photons to be sure. Gentlemen, limestone provides a great environment for cyanobacteria because of its reflective properties."

Hooten's terminology and explanation fell on nonprofessional ears, yet Chief Jefferson understood enough to suggest, "So, what you're saying is, there's a natural light source inside the cavern, right?"

"Yes, sir."

Pete spoke up, "Mr. Hooten, I could use your help. Would you be willing to dive with me today?

Hooten's answer surprised both men, "No, sir, I will not. I have no desire to dive with you or anyone else. Mr. Colucci, I have never strapped on a scuba tank and don't ever plan to. In my professional opinion, the water is for aquatics and the land is reserved for us monkeys… if you get my drift."

"I understand," Pete said, then informed the Chief, "Okay, I'm going down. You two monkeys keep talking but if I'm not back in about twenty minutes, and since Mr. Hooten doesn't scuba dive, then I expect you to come down to save my ass."

Jefferson responded, "Colucci, my friend; you are up shit creek. I can't even swim."

"Wonderful," Pete mumbled, despairingly. Adjusting the diving mask for comfort, Pete waded in waist-deep and then dove for the depths.

Hooten asked the Chief, "Was that a rebel flag on the back of his tank?"

"Afraid so."

* * * * *

The lake water still amazed Pete, the deeper he dove the purer it seemed, like bottled water, and cold, the iciness felt through his diving suit. And the deeper he dove, the more doubtful he became. About 50 feet was his limit, but now, with at least another 50 feet tacked on to his limit, skepticism fringed on flat-out fear. He was too old for this, Pete knew it, yet the thought of another adventure was like calling a sloppy bluff in poker.

Playing the odds; taking too many dumb chances and not proving anything to anybody other than himself, he dove on, slowly, eventually reaching the clear indigo bottom. Plant life flourished, unusual at this depth in a lake. And that radiant light inside the cavern, an illumination likened to fluorescent tubes. Hooten had clarified the light source as an acceptable theory since no other rationalization existed. The deputy divers were nowhere in sight, having entered the cavern ten minutes before Pete's arrival. Pete hesitated outside the mouth of the cavern, using his fins to remain stationary, his body weights not doing the trick. Second thoughts tested his mettle.

'What the hell am I doing? Is this stupid dive for Chief Jefferson, or me? I must be out of my mind, this is dangerous, I have a daughter, she needs me. I could resurface, tell the sheriff I got cramps, or that I was sick, or that my tank was malfunctioning. But would he believe me? Would Hooten and the paramedic believe me? And the two divers, would they believe me, laugh at me, treat me like an old fool? Better an old fool than a dead fool. 'Special assistant' my ass. Every idiot in this fiasco is being paid except for me.'

Pete decided to withdraw, give up the hunt, no longer willing to face the unknown, life was just too precious to throw it away trying to prove that he 'still had it', still a purposeful man, still the young warrior he was in Vietnam yet never would be again. He didn't have to prove anything to anyone, including himself.

Pete gave a strong kick with his right fin to begin his ascent but stopped immediately as a figure approached the mouth of the cave from inside. What Pete saw sent his stomach into spasms; he almost puked into his regulator.

One of the St. Johns County divers floated toward the front of the cave, the primary regulatory out of his mouth, the gushing air bubbles slowly propelling his body forward. A large pinkish cloud followed the body, the arms motionless. The diver's body hit one side of the cavern; the contact caused what was left of the man to invert. As the pink cloud caught up and obscured the body, Pete briefly saw blood pouring from his entrails and body cavity, the legs were gone, hips, and genitals, were all gone, tank straps dangling like tensile. Then nothing could be seen but a pinkish cloud with a bright red center.

The non-decompression depth is one hundred feet depending on the length of a dive, Pete knew that, but now he didn't care. To suffer decompression illness was preferable to be bitten in half by whatever lurked deep within the cavern. He kicked his fins into overdrive. The whereabouts of the other diver never crossed his mind.

CHAPTER 11

Chief Jefferson and Ron Hooten were still engaged in small talk when Pete emerged from beneath the lake like an underwater nuclear missile. He threw off his face mask, gasped for air, then swam a short distance to the bank. Both men helped Pete out of the water. Panting like a worn-out old hunting dog, he bent over as if to puke.

The Chief first thought '*He's having a heart attack*' and yelled at the paramedic, "McMurphy, get the hell over here!"

McMurphy sprang like a jackrabbit out of the patio chair. He opened the fence gate and ran to the three men. He pushed Chief Jefferson aside and grasped Pete by his left arm, "Sir, are you okay?"

Pete had no time for pity. He placed the palm of his left hand on McMurphy's chest and pushed him back. "Get away from me!" Pete screamed, still wheezing.

Jefferson attempted to calm down Pete, "It's okay, Colucci, he's just trying to help. What's wrong?"

"What's wrong? WHAT'S WRONG?" Pete

yelled, straightening his posture. "One of your divers has been bitten in half! That's what's wrong!"

"Jesus," Jefferson muttered. "Where's the other diver?"

Pete stared at the lawman for a moment. "Hell, if I know!" he finally yelled. "Maybe in the stomach of a big turtle, air tanks and all, hell, you go down there and find him!"

The Chief asked the stupidest of questions, "Are you sure the deputy was dead?"

Pete responded more in anger than knowledge, and without tact. "Are you an idiot? The man's bitten in half! Yeah, he's dead!"

Hooten inquired, "How do you know the turtle did it?"

"WHAT?" Pete screamed; his patience drained. "HOOTEN, IT WASN'T A DAMN GREAT WHITE! I CAN TELL YOU THAT!"

"Calm down, Colucci," Chief Jefferson said softly. "YOU CALM DOWN!"

"Okay, okay," Jefferson replied, looking at the paramedic, "Do you need to recover the body for…."

The paramedic answered before Jefferson could finish, "How?"

"Good question," Jefferson replied. "I guess we could get a diver to go down and…."

"WELL, IT AIN'T GONNA BE ME!" Pete immediately advised.

"I didn't mean…" the Chief hesitated, then said, "Okay, let's all calm down and figure out this thing. We have to…"

Something emerged near the bank. All four men jumped back, from fear, not caution. Middleton, the second diver, took off his mask and flip-flopped ashore. He stopped in front of the three men, fumbled with his face mask, kept his head down as if crestfallen, and acted unaffected, but his unruffled demeanor was refuted by trembling hands.

"Middleton?" Jefferson said gently, speculating that the deputy was in shock.

"Yeah," Middleton replied, not looking up.

"Look at me," Jefferson said. Middleton raised his head. A face seemingly bleached pale, bluish lips, enlarged pupils the size of two quarters.

McMurphy, the paramedic, stated the obvious, "He's in shock."

The Chief stared at McMurphy with a chilly gaze, as if telling the man not to say another word. McMurphy complied, not saying another word. Jefferson continued, "Middleton, do you feel like talking?"

"Yeah," he answered, meekly, as if drugged.

"What happened down there?"

"Burke's dead."

"Yeah, Colucci told us. What happened?"

"The turtle got him. I hid in a crevice. I saw it all.

Burke didn't stand a chance. It was huge, the thing was huge." Middleton lowered his head.

Hooten asked, "How big?"

Middleton looked up. "Who are you?"

Hooten replied, "Ron Hooten, sir. I'm a herpetologist from the University of Florida. A turtle expert."

Middleton calmly said, "A turtle expert." Not as a question, but as a clarifying statement.

"Yes, sir. Can you describe what you saw, and how big it was?"

"It was a turtle, a big one, the size of a school bus, but wider and longer."

"Can you describe the carapace?"

"The what?"

"The shell, sir."

"It was a turtle shell."

"Smooth, leathery, any dorsal ridges, patterns around its eyes?"

Middleton stared at Hooten as if contemplating homicide, then suddenly burst out in anger. "How the fuck would I know! My partner was bitten in half right in front of me, so I didn't exactly have time to take any God-damned notes!"

Jefferson attempted to calm the situation. "Okay, take it easy, Middleton." Then Jefferson told the paramedic. "Get him to the hospital."

Middleton said, "No," before the paramedic could respond.

The Chief still tried to console. "Listen, you need to…."

Middleton raised his head. "NO, God damn it! I know his wife and kids, we had cookouts together, he was my friend, and I'm not leaving him down there!"

Pete said, "He was at the mouth of the cavern, why didn't you bring…"

Middleton interrupted, "Well, he's not now. Maybe he floated away, maybe he… hell, I don't know, I just wanted to get away in case…" Middleton paused, bewildered, incredulous, sick to his stomach. "I'm going back in to get him."

Chief Jefferson responded, "No, you're not going back in."

Pete spoke up. "Middleton, that's not a good idea."

Middleton cut his eyes toward Pete. "Where were you? You were supposed to be down there… where were you?"

"I made it as far as the mouth of the cavern. That's when I saw, well, I saw your friend."

Burke's remains buoyed to the surface. Hooten saw it first. "Oh, sweet Jesus," he muttered.

Burke's air tanks were empty, the regulator no longer bubbling, his weight belt chewed off with the first bite, his body sapped of blood and no longer pooling in the water; fish nibbled on his innards.

Middleton said quietly, "I'll go get him."

Pete advised, "Don't go back out there, Middleton."

Jefferson also tried to discourage the man, "We'll get Burke. You need to…"

Middleton's voice was threatening. "Who, Chief? Which one of you wants to go out there to get him? You?" Then he looked at Pete, "You?" Middleton turned to reenter the water while warning, "Don't nobody try to stop me, or I'll kill you." Nobody tried.

* * * * *

After throwing up his morning breakfast upon seeing the grisly remains, the paramedic bagged the body, backed up his EMT vehicle in the empty lot next to Pete's property, then loaded Burke's corpse, what was left of it. Middleton had jumped into the back of the vehicle to escort his friend to the morgue. Still in shock, according to the paramedic, but still refusing medical attention, still daring anyone to stop him. Nobody tried.

As the vehicle pulled away, Hooten said, "Gentlemen, I need to examine the remains, with the coroner's permission, so I will be leaving. But I'll venture a guess at what may be down there. It sounds like an Archelon-type specimen, which means…"

"A what?" Jefferson questioned, then added, "Speak English."

"Fine. Archelon is extinct or thought to be. Its sister group of Protostegidae may be another option to...."

"English," Jefferson repeated.

"Very well. Archelon is the biggest turtle ever documented, a good sixteen feet from head to tail and approximately right at five thousand pounds. Paleontologists have found at least five specimens and believe..."

"From around here?" Jefferson queried.

"No, sir. North and South Dakota, from the Pierre Shale along the Cheyenne and Sheyenne Rivers. The biggest one, given the nickname "Brigitta", was unearthed in Oglala Lakota County in South Dakota. It's on display at the Natural History Museum in Vienna."

Jefferson muttered, "North and South Dakota," disbelievingly.

Pete said, "Vienna?"

Hooten replied to Pete, "Yes, sir, Vienna, Austria." Then replied to Jefferson. "And, yes, North and South Dakota. Gentlemen, what we call America was underwater millions of years ago and Florida spent most of her life under the sea, but I can't honestly say that Archelon was 'THE' biggest turtle, it's just the biggest one ever found."

Pete asked, "Are you suggesting we have a prehistoric turtle on our hands?"

Hooten responded, "Suggesting? No, sir, it's more like a wild guess. Let's just call it 'Snapper' to avoid the guesswork. Sir, the remains of an unknown species of dinosaur were recently discovered in Argentina. Lost civilizations are still excavated or discovered. The human species would like to think we know it all, but we don't, this old globe has been rotating for billions of years. There's no telling what remains to be discovered."

Jefferson was more to the point. "So, if we have a prehistoric turtle swimming around in Florida lakes or rivers or sleeping under the Jacksonville pier, how could it have lived that long without anyone seeing it before?"

"Sleeping under a pier," Hooten repeated, "That's a good word for it, 'sleeping.' Chief, the scientific locution is brumating. It's believed that the Archelon or her sister group of Protostegidia may have been able to brumate underwater in a dormant state for… for God knows how long."

Pete suggested, "Turtles breathe, they need oxygen."

Hooten countered, "Most do. But prehistoric turtles from the Cretaceous age, maybe before and after, are believed to have had the capacity to cover themselves with mud or sea floor and go to sleep, to brumate, possibly for years. Cloacal respiration helps them survive."

Jefferson interrupted, "English, Hooten, English."

Hooten replied, "Oh, sorry, Chief. Well, cutaneous respiration is common among turtles, frogs, sea snakes, salamanders…."

Jefferson interrupted again, slightly irritated. "Hooten, what the hell are you talking about? What is this colloquial respiration?"

Hooten smiled before answering. "Colloquial, that's funny. The word, Chief, is cloacal. During hibernation, turtles can breathe through their butts."

Pete said, "You're kidding, right?"

Hooten replied, "Nope, they can breathe through their butts."

Pete muttered, mostly to himself, "Talk about bad breath."

Jefferson doubted every word. "Okay, fine, this turtle we have on our hands can breathe through its ass. But for millions of years? It would rot!"

"Perhaps," Hooten replied. "I'd speculate something that big is capable of brumating, or an unknown category of hibernation or suspended animation, for perhaps hundreds of years, maybe more. The African Lungfish can go into a state of suspended animation for three to five years. It needs no food or water; it doesn't urinate or make waste. A lot of our commonly known animals hibernate, like snakes, turtles, ground squirrels…"

"Bears," Pete added.

"No, sir, they don't," Hooten countered. "Most people think bears hibernate, but they're just light sleepers."

Chief Jefferson asked, "How does an animal stay alive for any length of time in hibernation or suspended animation?"

Hooten replied, "Well, just like a light sleeping bear, they eat a ton of food before going into suspended animation or the less demanding act of hibernation. It's fat, a lot of fat, it nourishes their system while they sleep, hibernate, or whatever."

Jefferson ventured, "So, you believe we have a creature… this, this Snapper as you suggested, that's been around for hundreds of years, sleeping his fat-ass off until he ran out of fat?"

Shrugging his shoulders, Hooten replied, "I'm just suggesting, Chief, that's the best I can do. Gentlemen, I must leave. I want to be sure I chat with the coroner before he starts guessing at the cause of death. I'll talk to you later, gentlemen."

As Hooten walked away, Jefferson asked Pete, "Do you believe this shit?"

"No," Pete replied. "But I guess it's possible, I don't know, and I don't think Hooten knows."

Jefferson changed the subject. "Did you notice your neighbors across the lake?"

"No."

"There were three of them watching the dive.

When the body surfaced, they scrambled like spooked chickens back to their homes. They saw it… we got a problem."

"WE, got a problem?" Pete countered. "What exactly do you mean by, WE?"

Chief Jefferson smirked, then said, "Sounds like you're already burned out with police work, Colucci."

The time had arrived for Pete to state the obvious. "I'm already burned out?" he restated. "I'm not a cop; I'm an old man trying to be relevant past his prime. Yeah, I saw bad things in Nam, but so what? I was a young gung-ho dumbass with thoughts of glory, no way would I get killed, but the longer I live the more I thank God every day for this precious gift called life. I puked when I saw the girls' legs; I almost puked in my regulator when I saw the diver's body, and that was after I'd already decided to get my ass outa the lake and call it quits.

"I was scared shitless; I no longer have what it takes to be brave, to dare death, to ever again think that I'm invincible. A special assistant my ass! How would you explain a civilian getting killed in the line of duty if it isn't even his duty to do so? They'd crucify you on the cross for dumbass cops. What the hell do you want from me, Chief?"

"Damn," Jefferson replied. "That was a hell of a speech."

Pete had had it. "Fuck you, Jefferson," he said, then started to walk around the lawman.

"Wait a minute," Jefferson said, grabbing Pete's left arm.

Pete pulled his arm away quickly. "Get your hands off me!" he demanded.

"Okay, okay," Jefferson said, almost in a whisper. "Sorry, okay? Colucci, I apologize, you are relevant, and I need you."

"Aw, bullshit," Pete swore. "For what, Jefferson, what do you need me for?" Pete had dropped all courtesy, no longer was it 'Chief', it was 'Jefferson', man-to-man, no quarter given.

Jefferson hesitated; the truth stuck in his throat. "Colucci," he finally replied, quietly, almost inaudibly. "I'm dying, stage four, my time is limited. No doubt this will be my last case and I'm desperate. Maybe I want to go out in a blaze of glory, solving a case with a big turtle as the culprit which sounds screwy as hell, but that's what we're facing here. I don't want to fail. Yes, I'm using you when I shouldn't, but I don't trust the St. Augustine deputies and they don't trust me, that's also what we're facing here. I can't swim and my two deputies don't scuba dive, you popped up outa the water all decked out in a wetsuit two days ago full of piss and vinegar, so I thought, hell, why not? Why not ask this nosey old man to help me? Recruiting you was all self-centered, I played you for a sap. I'm sorry."

"Damn," Pete replied, recalling the deaths of his wife and sister from the monster called cancer. "That was a hell of a speech."

Chief Jefferson managed a weak grin. "Yeah, I'm not very good at speeches, I'm used to barking orders like an old bloodhound, but at least we got what we wanted to say off our chests."

"There ya go," Pete replied. "Using that word 'we' again."

Jefferson stuck out his hand, Pete accepted the handshake as the Chief said, "Thanks, Colucci, I'll leave you alone now. We weren't that bad of a team, were we?"

Pete broke the handshake. "We still are."

CHAPTER 12

The Chief, Pete, and Professor of Herpetology Ron Hooten met at the New St. Francis Police Station late that evening. Hooten had requested a private meeting with Chief Jefferson only, but the last couple of days had taken a toll on the old lawman. He wasn't feeling well, cancer draining his energy and life; hence a quick invitation to his 'special assistant' to attend the meeting. Pete was back on 'the team' and was willing to help.

The town of New St. Francis resembled an isolated territory in the days of the Old West; an old hardware and gun store, one old family-owned grocery store, an old brick schoolhouse with old desks, and a couple of old hunting and fishing equipment shops that doubled as gossip clubs. Most of the townsfolk were old. The town reeked of old.

Younger generations lived in outlying residential areas or labored on nearby farms. Everybody knew everybody. Hitching posts were still utilized for horse lovers; a scent of horse manure wafted around the town square. A few residents were licensed to carry, but most people packed some sort of weapon. Gun racks adorned the back window of pickup trucks; rifles, shotguns, and AR-15s on full display.

The 'oldness' of New St. Francis attracted a breed of new residents unhappy with the newness of America, yet for travelers off the beaten path the 'oldness' was a novelty for jokes or a couple of photos. The residents tolerated travelers and possible customers during business hours but preferred them gone with the setting sun.

The New St. Francis Police Station was a two-story dilapidated old building with an inside scaffold, only used once to hang an innocent man, and never used thereafter. The four old cells were grubby, damp, and rarely utilized. The office was small, with three desks, the biggest one claimed by the Chief. No privacy except for a clean but old tiny bathroom with a leaky faucet. A messy dispatcher's desk was in front; no rails, no divider, nothing to block unwanted access to the three desks in back in front of the cells.

The one dispatcher worked an eight-to-five day; no overtime was authorized. Overnight calls rolled over to the cellphone of whichever officer was on night duty. A small window air-conditioner vibrated noisily, keeping the police station adequately cooled. The outside red brick was crumbling and had been for years.

The Chief sat behind his desk. Pete and Hooten pulled up the two deputy chairs to begin the meeting.

Chief Jefferson began the meeting. "Hooten, you requested this get-together. What's on your mind?"

"A lot," Hooten responded. "The coroner has ruled the diver's death as an accident. He…"

"Bullshit," Pete interrupted.

Hooten replied, "Afraid so, Mister Colucci. I implied an aquatic animal may have killed the man, but the coroner looked at me like I was an idiot. He's familiar with alligator bites, shark bites, and the normal animal injuries in the area, but he's not going to accept anything other than a horrific accident, with the 'slight possibility' of an alligator attack. In other words, he's covering his ass."

Jefferson suggested, "Middleton saw it. That's proof."

Hooten disagreed. "A traumatized deputy in shock? No, Chief, that dog don't hunt. Who else has seen it?" He looked at Pete. "You, Mister Colucci, did you see it, or thought you saw it?"

"I think I saw its head pop up in the lake," Pete answered.

"Think you saw it? That's another dog that don't hunt," then Hooten returned his attention to the Chief. "Have you or your deputies run a missing person's report, or file, whatever kind of information you folks use about missing people around here?"

The Chief misunderstood. "We're still looking for Miss Barnes's boyfriend, but no luck yet."

"I'm not referring to him," Hooten said. "I have a gut instinct the poor man is most likely turtle feces by now. On a hunch, I contacted the University of Florida and they in turn contacted the Alachua County Sheriff's Office in Gainesville to ask them to run a missing person's report generated from on or near any body of water in the general vicinity. The report is alarming."

Chief Jefferson said, "Go on."

Hooten pulled out a folded faxed sheet, unfolded it, then said, "Here's the information they faxed me to the coroner's office," and he began reading. "Last week the police in Crescent City received a report of an incident that occurred at the south end of Crescent Lake in the Crescent Lake Conservation Area. The area is big and swampy, in many places of unknown depth. A naturalist went exploring where he shouldn't be exploring and ended up missing. A search party found his boots with his feet still in them." Hooten looked up. "Sound familiar?" he asked Jefferson.

Jefferson replied, "One incident, or is there more?"

"Yes, sir, there is," Hooten replied, then continued his reading. "Last month in the Horseshoe Point Conservation Area a mile or so below Palatka, two teenage boys went canoeing where they shouldn't be canoeing and came up missing. The area is dense vegetation, marshy, and shallow except for one sinkhole, the depth unknown. All they found during a search was a busted-up canoe stained with blood, two paddles floating nearby, and a cooler full of beer."

Pete said, "So, you're thinking this could be our Snapper?"

Hooten said, "I have one more incident to read, then I'll answer your question." He continued, "Lake George in Putnam County is fed by the St. Johns River, the lake is huge, shallow, except for a sinkhole that's never been explored. At the northern end of Lake George is Drayton Island, privately owned, eleven miles long and seven miles wide. The island has a few residents and is only accessible by ferry. There's also a good-sized lake in the middle of Drayton Island that's never been fully explored. The entire island is heavily covered in foliage and undergrowth, and the ground is soggy. During the plantation and steamboat era, seven slaves and a few tourists disappeared at different times. Very few remains were found; the local authorities attributed the deaths to wild animals. Several months ago, two people went snorkeling where they shouldn't be snorkeling in the island's isolated lake. Call the snorkelers brave or stupid, it doesn't matter, they haven't been heard from since." Hooten refolded the faxed paper.

Chief Jefferson still wanted more, "What else?"

"Chief," Hooten began. "People and animals have been missing for years all along the St. Johns River, some from accidents, but many listed simply as 'missing' with no explanation. There have been a few reports of big turtles over the years, but most, if not all the reports, were ignored as fairy tales by attention-seeking losers or booze or candidates for insane asylums. No evidence, so, therefore, the cases were closed. Gentlemen, the St. Johns River dumps into the Atlantic northwest of Jacksonville where freshwater mixes with seawater, so I hate to tell you this, but our Alligator snapper, or Archelon, or whatever this thing may be, is most likely a Euryhaline."

Pete said, "A what?"

"An Euryhaline, Mr. Colucci. They can survive in saltwater and freshwater."

Jefferson stated, "I didn't know animals could live in both."

Hooten grinned. "Yes, sir, you do, but you don't think about it. Take salmon as an example, they live their lives in the sea and then at the end of their lives swim up freshwater streams to spawn. Herring, frogs, snakes, and ells; are all Euryhalines. Even Bull Sharks have been spotted in the St. Johns River. Sea turtles cannot live long in freshwater, but just about every other species of turtle can live in both ecosystems."

Pete ventured, "Like an Alligator Snapper."

Hooten replied, "Yes, and especially an Archelon or one of its cousins."

Befuddled, Chief Jefferson stammered, "Wait,

wait a minute or two here. So, what you're saying is that our turtle could eat his lunch, then go out to sea to digest his catch, is that correct?"

Hooten replied, "Our turtle can go out to sea anytime it wants."

"Jesus," Pete swore. "How do we stop this thing, I mean, how do we catch it or kill it?"

Hooten shook his head. "I don't know, Mr. Colucci, that's out of my pay grade. I wish we could catch it. I'd love to study it, find out what caused this freak of nature, or if indeed we are dealing with what was thought to be extinct. It killed humans; humans normally kill what kills them. We must catch it or kill it because ignoring this beast is not an option."

The window air-conditioner stopped the constant vibrating and started shaking hard enough to rattle the top window. A trivial hum returned for a second then quit as the shaking and rattling increased. "Excuse me," Jefferson said, embarrassed. Arising from his chair, Jefferson took three steps to the air-conditioner and pounded it twice on top with his fist. The air-conditioner stopped shaking and returned to its normally loud vibrating. "We've been allocated funds for a new one," Jefferson lied, returning to his chair. Sitting down, he asked Hooten, "So, how do we do what we have to do without creating a public panic?"

Hooten dodged a solution. "Sir, that is far above

my pay grade, too. I think that problem is in your job description."

Pete asked, "I don't understand how something this large can avoid detection, I mean, someone must have seen it, don't you think?"

"Mr. Colucci, when you sit or stand by the lake you see turtles, right?"

"Yeah."

"If one pops its nose above the surface for air and it's near you, it's fine as long as you don't move. If you move, the turtle goes back under immediately, right?"

Yeah."

"If one is basking in the sun and you walk up on it, it darts like a bullet back into the water, right?"

"Yeah."

"Turtles spook easily. My guess is our big boy in your lake does its hunting at night to avoid all the noises of this modern world, and maybe back in the old days a steamboat could easily spook it. Before then, who knows? I'm only guessing." He looked at Chief Jefferson. "Do you have a plan, sir?"

Before Chief Jefferson could reply, the St. Augustine Sheriff's diver, Middleton, opened the door and walked in. Pale, still looking distraught, he stood next to Chief Jeffersons' desk as if in a stupor. All three men considered the deputy too sick and distressed to be driving a vehicle or walking the streets.

Hooten spoke first. "Middleton, you said you

were going to the hospital when you left the coroner's office. Did you?"

"I lied," he responded. Then told Chief Jefferson, "I know how to kill this thing."

CHAPTER 13

Sheriff's deputy and diver Mike Middleton's family roots were deeply embedded in survival beneath the sea. His grandfather served in WWII as a Navy 'frogman', technically known as UDT's (Underwater Demolition Teams), divers who swam ashore to recon beaches before Allied invasions. During the invasion of Normandy, 91 frogmen had been killed or wounded on Omaha Beach. Middleton's grandfather was one of the survivors. His father served in Vietnam as a young graduate from the budding Navy Seal program started in 1962. As a Navy Seal/frogman, he reconnoitered South Vietnam's waterways for their accessibility to boats of the Brown Water Navy, especially in IV Corps, the murky Mekong Delta.

His father also participated in executions of mid-level Viet Cong cadre. Mike had carried on the family tradition by joining the Navy as a frogman, but after the Navy phased out frogmen in 1983 and sent all active-duty divers to the Navy Seals, he decided to serve out his enlistment and leave the Navy for a career in law enforcement as a scuba diver. The Seals' professionalism and Mike's independent free spirit didn't mentally harmonize. After twenty-nine years with the St. Augustine Sheriff's Department, his retirement and a chartered deep fishing boat business dream were four months away from becoming a reality.

Mike Middleton was in great shape for a man in his sixties; slim and muscular, scuba diving had kept his body in shape and his mind sharp. A tall man, 6'3", permanent five o'clock shadow, dark hair with a slightly receding hairline, charitable and affable to a fault. He'd recovered a lot of bodies from the deep, mostly swimming and boating accidents, but had never stomached the loss of a fellow driver on the job, especially Burke's grisly death. Middleton's emotional well-being suffered; his rage was tough to control.

Middleton's voice was too loud for the small jail, but the three men listening to his scheme didn't interrupt, perhaps exhibiting a measure of condolence for the loss of his buddy, perhaps out of self-preservation. Middleton was wearing his deputy outfit, gray with black stripes, but the 9mm Glock holstered on his belt looked intimidating being worn by a distraught lawman who could be borderline PTSD and filled with rage.

His plan for killing the killer turtle sounded simple, bait it into the cavern, seal off both ends then let it depart this life hungry. Executing the idea, however, presented a nightmare of risk, cooperation from several divers, the participation from his brother-in-law's construction company, large commercial air-conditioning vents, and above all, strict security so as not to panic the public. Chief Jefferson's two deputies had managed to assuage the fears of the three neighbors who saw Burke's severed body surface on the lake. The deputies told a tale easy for Floridians to believe: a large alligator killed the unfortunate diver; professional divers were going to kill it.

While listening to the details of Middleton's plan, Pete thought, *"There's no way I'm getting involved in this stupid plan,"* while Hooten assumed the deputy was suffering from extreme shock and the possible mental collapse from witnessing a giant turtle snap his buddy into two pieces. Chief Jefferson, however, with few if any resolutions, listened intently, desperate to end this thing before more people were killed or injured, or his cancer knocked him out of the game permanently.

One option considered then disregarded by Middleton's diving buddies was using spear guns tipped with high explosives, but to get that close meant certain death for a diver. His associates had agreed to act as guards with armed spear guns to hopefully protect the divers involved in trapping Snapper, but enthusiastic volunteers were few. Middleton first solicited help from the St. Augustine Sheriff's divers then called a short list of professional divers he trusted.

Enraged by the loss of Burke, the few hands

raised to volunteer belonged to divers from the Sheriff's office; only one civilian diver volunteered, but the rest assumed that Middleton had lost his mind.

Middleton's strategy was to bait Snapper with a large carcass, a cow or horse, bloody raw to leave a powerful scent and place it mid-way inside the cavern. When Snapper was trapped inside, three concrete trucks on both ends of the cavern would pour tons of cement into the vents from above to both entrances in front of the cavern.

Pete argued that concrete takes at least 12 to 24 hours to set properly, implying that Snapper could easily worm his way out. Middleton told Pete that his brother-in-law owned a construction company, so Middleton knew the ins and outs of concrete. Whereas standard Portland cement normally takes a good day to set, rapid-hardening hydraulic cement can set in as little as two hours.

Pete scoffed at that suggestion, too, stating the divers wouldn't have two hours, and that to put them in Harm's Way by such a method amounted to suicide. Middleton negated Pete's view, informing him, Hooten, and Chief Jefferson that an improved top-secret military version of rapid hardening hydraulic cement set almost immediately, used exclusively by Navy Seals working from submarines. There were tons of the top-secret hydraulic cement stored at the Jacksonville Naval Air Station.

Hooten didn't like the plan and shook his head, marginally, not wanting to offend Middleton. Pete thought the idea was half-baked with no chance of ever being fully baked. Jefferson was middle-of-the-road baffled, unable to approve or disapprove, knowing time was critical, his options few, but not wanting to waste lives on a desperate scheme.

Middleton asked the obvious. "Well, gentlemen, are you with me or against me?" Only silence. "Hell, say something!"

Hooten spoke up. "Middleton, are you up to this?"

Middleton responded, "Are you?" Hooten didn't reply.

The Chief asked, "How long would it take you to put this plan together?"

"It's already in the works."

Jefferson asked, "You did all this in one afternoon?"

"I did," Middleton replied. "We hope to start the operation by tomorrow afternoon."

"Has the Sheriff approved of this plan?"

"He's at a sheriff's conference in New Orleans."

Jefferson persisted, "I repeat, has he approved this plan?"

Middleton remained evasive. "I talked to him, yeah."

"Answer my question," Jefferson demanded. "Did he approve?"

Middleton told the truth. "Nope, he wants me to wait until he gets back, that's three days away. Chief, do you want to wait that long?" Jefferson paused; Middleton repeated, "Do you?"

The Chief knew they had to act, to do something, if Snapper was in the swamp, then they had to act immediately. "No, I think we better do something while we have the chance."

Pete had heard enough. "Wait a minute, Middleton, let's talk this thing through. Even if feasible, we don't know where the other end of the cavern opens, probably in the swamp behind The Refuge community, maybe not, and we don't even know the length of the damn thing or if Snapper will be in the cavern or the swamp. Have you thought about those things?"

Middleton surprised all three men. "Police choppers will take turns over the swamp all day and night, staying at high altitude so as not to spook Snapper. They're equipped with infrared equipment once the sun sets. They're already dropping small bait, dead chickens, ducks, roadkill, anything to draw or trick Snapper into the swamp or to stay in the swamp. I believe it's still there. We'll know soon."

"Fine," Pete casually agreed. "But where's the other end of the cavern, or tunnel, whatever?"

"That's where you and I come in handy."

Pete blinked, then asked, "Say what?"

"White can't dive, his finger is infected. You and

I are the only ones who have seen or been inside the cavern. We are going to explore its length, time is crucial."

Pete couldn't believe the audacity he had just heard. "The hell you say!"

"The hell I did say. You and me, my friend… excuse me, I meant to say the Chief's 'special assistant', we are going in.'

Pete glanced at Jefferson, Jefferson shrugged his shoulders, and Hooten snickered. Placing his left elbow on the armchair, Pete put his forehead in his left hand, rubbed his temples, aware he had promised Jefferson his continued collaboration, then said, "When?"

Middleton replied, "Daybreak."

CHAPTER 14:
WALKER'S LAST WALK

The middle child of nine children via impoverished parents, William Brown was born with a speech impediment, a slow mental aptitude, and defective growth hormones. The kids mocked him as 'Babbling Bill' due to his short-pause speech impairment, and teased him incessantly as they grew taller, but Bill didn't. His parents managed to place Bill in a school for special needs children on his tenth birthday, then packed their bags and the other eight kids and skipped town without leaving a forwarding address. Foster homes without hugs or compassion became the norm.

As an adult, Bill managed to hold down odd jobs for a month or two before walking off without notice to search for his next employment opportunity. Jobs seemed bothersome, boring, and unnecessary after making a few bucks. He was gifted at one thing: walking. Bill loved to walk, able to walk for miles upon miles without breaking a sweat or losing his breath.

A nomad his entire life, and born an intransigent Floridian in its tropical climate, Bill never saw the need for a permanent home with all its expensive up-keep and damnable property taxes.

A home could be anything: a cardboard box, a self-built shelter, or an old pup tent, and restrooms with clean water were available in convenience stores, restaurants, and grocery stores; restrooms were every-where, with free bars of soap or containers of liquid soap, plus paper or cloth towels for drying.

He shared a pup tent with a homeless woman once, thought they were in love, or what he consid-ered love, but within two weeks, she was gone, nev-er to return. Heartbroken, unable to grasp why she would desert him like his parents had, Bill moved on from one secluded deep-woods location to many se-cluded spots until local authorities no longer consid-ered his homes as secluded.

At the age of 32, Bill had found his private para-dise: a swampy, almost inaccessible location of thick vegetation and total privacy adjacent to a community called The Refuge.

Cardboard boxes were passe, as were pup tents or shabby self-built shelters. Bill had pilfered enough pallet wood to build a dwelling set on concrete blocks with plywood for a floor covered with carpeting from dumpster-diving. An old, screened window allowed a breeze if a breeze blew, and a battery-operated fan provided a fake breeze when needed. Canned food was stored in one corner; a mattress found on the side of the road provided a bed. Thick, ratty blankets or bedcovers from a dumpster provided warmth in winter. Bill was happy with his 'lakefront' property.

He wondered if the man at Outback had really seen what Bill had seen, only once, but once was enough. A monster turtle had moseyed by his pallet home a month or so back, totally indifferent to the worm observing its movements. Fear was not a factor; neither Bill nor the turtle was worried about the other; live and let live.

Bill had settled in for the steamy night, the battery-operated fan humming at full blast, the screened window wide open. A vibration rattled his pallet home. The ground trembled as if a minor earthquake had struck northeast Florida.

"What... the... hell," Bill stammered to himself. He opened the plywood door and scrambled outside. Hot and muggy, but with a full moon that lit the area like a nightlight. Bill looked up. "Oh... it's... you," he said to his buddy turtle.

His five-ton buddy turtle was hungry. It stretched its thick neck downward, closer to Bill.

"What... you... want... tonight?" he asked the turtle. The turtle withdrew its neck, posturing for a strike. Bill finally got the message. "Well... I... tired... anyway. Tired... of... movin'... tired... of... life."

The turtle struck. The Walker had walked his last walk.

CHAPTER 15

A predictable Florida July morning, steamy and sticky, humidity abated just a bit from sporadic rain during the night to fashion a slow-moving eerie fog over the lake. Visibility was a hit-and-miss dynamic; the fog was thick as cotton in places, cigarette-smoke thin in others, with a trivial breeze less powerful than a baby's breath.

Middleton and Pete checked and double-checked their diving equipment. Two other divers from the St. Augustine Sheriff's Department stood behind them. They would wait outside the cavern in case of an emergency, although neither diver had the slightest idea what they could do or should do if this thing, this Snapper, this supposedly giant turtle the size of a cabin cruiser attacked or showed up or decided Pete and Middleton were a suitable breakfast. The same paramedic sat in the same lawn chair sipping coffee. Chief Jefferson had yet to arrive.

Pete was not a happy camper, nor an enthusiastic scuba diver. His mood had soured overnight, bravado having slipped away, his expectation of success lower than a snake's belly in a wagon wheel rut. "I can't believe I'm doing this crap," he complained, looking into the fog banks drifting across the lake. "It could be out there in the fog, just waiting for us."

"The fog will burn off by the time we get back," Middleton said.

"Yeah, if we do get back."

Middleton grinned. "You scared, Colucci?"

"Aren't you?" Pete shot back, returning his gaze to his diving partner. "You get paid for this, I don't. I'm doing this out of respect for Jefferson, nothing more. Hell, you and I both know I'm nothing but a screwball golden-age warrior trying to prove he's still got it, whatever the hell 'it' is. Jefferson calls me his 'special assistant'. What a crock! One of us will probably end up as a 'special snack' for Snapper. What I'm doing is illegal as hell, and you know it!"

Unruffled and under control, Middleton informed Pete, "You're a New St. Francis deputy, yeah, it's legal."

"Aw, bullshit, Middleton," Pete swore. "I'm not a deputy; I'm a prehistoric sucker."

"No," Middleton responded calmly. "You're a sworn-in deputy. Chief Jefferson has the paperwork to prove it. He swore you in two days ago."

"Jefferson never swore…" Pete stopped arguing. *'Of course,'* he thought. *'The Chief wasn't a fool, he has his ass covered, a fake deputy with fake paperwork; I'm the fool!'*

Middleton chuckled. "Are you getting the picture?"

Pete muttered, "That sneaky sonavabitch."

"He's using you to watch us, right?"

Pete came clean. "Yeah, I'm supposed to watch you guys. The Chief doesn't trust the St. Augustine deputies and apparently, you guys don't trust him. What is this, some type of rivalry or jealousy? What's going on here?"

Middleton came clean. "Colucci, ten years ago when Jefferson was still a lowly deputy, he shot a seventeen-year-old kid trying to siphon gas from a car in this neighborhood, The Refuge. The kid was armed, he went for his gun, but Jefferson beat him to the draw. Both got off a shot, but the kid's round was wildly off-target. Of course, Jefferson was better trained and aimed for mass. Jefferson nailed the kid in his chest. He died before an ambulance could even get here."

"Sounds like an authorized shooting," Pete said.

"It was ruled as such, but the kid was high on dope and booze and just got caught doing something stupid. He didn't need to siphon gas and why he did it we'll never know. He was also the son of a St. Augustine deputy."

"Oh," Pete muttered.

"Yeah," Middleton said. "There's been bad blood ever since."

"I'm surprised Jefferson's not here this morning."

"He'll show up."

"Okay, so what now?"

"We go in. You ready, Deputy Colucci?"

Pete sneered. "Yeah, let's do this."

* * * * *

The water was colder than in previous dives, but the four divers weren't concerned about the chill; they were more vexed over the possibility of becoming cadavers. Middleton entered the lake with two tanks on his back, Pete just one, with the Rebel flag painted on the back. Both agreed if Pete's air supply ran low, he would leave for the surface while Middleton continued the exploration, depending on the length of the cavern. The other two deputy divers had twin tanks, but both refused to explore the cavern. Armed with explosive-tipped spear guns, they were there for an emergency by the cavern's entrance, no further.

The illumination inside the cavern had not diminished. Steadily sloping upward, visibility appeared suitable at least to the first modest curve to the right, about 75 yards in. The armed divers stopped as expected just outside the mouth of the cavern, one on each side, the expressions in their eyes behind their masks exposing the awe when they realized the size of the cavern, of the strange light source, and the fear they felt. Middleton gave the two divers a 'thumbs-up', they returned the gesture, and then deputies Pete Colucci and Mike Middleton carefully and slowly entered to explore the unknown.

Pete still questioned the sanity of his contribution; Middleton questioned the chances of their survival, both of their hearts pounding like base drums from an overflow of adrenaline and anxiety. Middleton stopped about thirty yards in and ran his right-hand glove along deep scars in the limestone from too big of a turtle in too small of a cavern. Pete noticed the deep scars on the opposite side. He looked at the scars but didn't stroke the limestone. He estimated the cavern to be roughly 30 feet wide, meaning Snapper was at least the same width. Something touched his left shoulder. Panic petrified him. Turning around with air bubbles bellowing out of his regulator, he reached for his dive knife. Pete wasn't going down without a noble fight. He came face to face with Middleton.

Middleton's eyes were laughing; Pete gave him a gloved finger. Middleton motioned with his head to continue forward. They moved deeper into the cavern. Pete needed to pee. Not able to hold it, Pete did what he had to do, embarrassed, unaware that 90% of divers urinated in their wetsuits, the other 10% fib.

The limestone walls were scarred and pitted with crevices large enough to accommodate a grown man. One crevice the length of a shipping container but half the height caught Pete's eye. The opening was too small for something the size of Snapper, but a gator could slip in or out. Pete cautiously tried to peek inside. Darker than the cavern, Pete had to utilize his flashlight for better scrutiny. The interior was enormous, honey-combed on one side, more of a catacomb on the other. Spacious, deep, and lengthy, perhaps part of the main cavern years ago. Pete couldn't see the grotto's deep floor nor determine the depth. Schools of fish darted about, nothing big, no gators. He moved on, Middleton twenty feet ahead.

The limestone's porous composition had eroded over millions of years, creating wide cracks, hollows, small nooks, and large cavities, an abundance of underwater homes for underwater creatures. Fish weren't as numerous as expected, only small schools darting here, hiding there. Middleton rounded the slight curve to the right then stopped immediately; something had caught his attention. Pete followed suit; stopping behind Middleton, but Middleton motioned him forward with his right hand and pointed to the side of the cavern with his left. Pete moved forward, slowly.

A wide opening offered access to a mammoth indention in the limestone, deep and dim. Middleton shined his flashlight for better illumination. Big enough to accommodate Snapper, but no outlet other than the opening. No fish, no turtles, nothing. The two divers moved on.

The cavern straightened out, a long tunnel of limestone maybe two or three hundred yards long. Visibility dimmed deep inside the cavern yet regained visibility nearer the exit to the swamp. Pete checked his pressure gauge; enough air for perhaps ten or fifteen minutes before he had to turn back, but decided not to push his luck. Middleton was still in the lead; Pete tugged on Middleton's right fin to gain his attention. Middleton turned around. Pete pointed to his pressure gauge and then pointed his finger upwards, implying it was time to get the hell out of the cavern. Middleton gave a thumbs up. Pete motioned for him to follow; Middleton shook his head. With two tanks, he had enough air to reach the end of the cavern before turning back.

Pete didn't like the idea. He motioned again for Middleton to follow. Middleton shook his head, again. Pete wasn't going to have a useless hand debate with a grown man and experienced diver. He gave Middleton the thumbs-up; Middleton returned the gesture, Pete turned around and kicked for home, for air, for safety.

Middleton remained motionless, ogling towards the end of the cavern, the water was not as clear but clear enough to see a vague light at the exit. Second thoughts tested his mettle, a picture of Burke's corpse burning his brain, Burke's beastly demise egging him forward. He had enough air to finish the mission; he hoped Snapper didn't finish him.

* * * * *

Pete resurfaced near the bank and exited the water. Jefferson was waiting for him; the paramedic was still glued to the lawn chair. Pete removed his mask. "Glad you could make it," he greeted, his tone laced with irony.

Jefferson had had a bad night, was too queasy and in too much pain for any sleep and was in no mood for small talk. "What's going on down there?" he demanded.

"Well, the two divers are still guarding the cavern entrance like the loyal underwater stormtroopers they are, and Middleton is salting his ass for Snapper."

Not concerned about two underwater stormtroopers, Jefferson said, "Middleton's in the cavern alone?"

"Yep," Pete replied. Jefferson looked weak and sick, and Pete said so. "Chief, you don't look good. Are you okay?

"Just a bad night," the Chief lied, then continued his quizzing. "Why didn't you stay with Middleton?"

"I have one tank; Middleton has two, I tried to get him to leave but he wouldn't, it's that simple."

Jefferson nervously shifted his weight, "So if Snapper is in the swamp and goes inside the cavern, Middleton is history."

"Breakfast is more like it. I tried to get the spear

gun cowboys to go inside to protect Middleton, but after a few minutes of hand-signaling bullshit, I gave up. Whatever Middleton told his buddies in St. Augustine must have scared them half to death. And if the coroner showed them what was left of Burke, well, I guess we're lucky they even showed up this morning."

"You need to go back down there."

"No way, Chief," Pete countered, I'm almost out of air."

Persistent, Jefferson stated, "You probably have enough air to relieve one of the deputies, switch tanks, he comes up, and you go inside with two tanks."

Unable to fathom Jefferson's idea, Pete responded, "Jefferson, you're out of your friggin' mind!"

Jefferson suggested, "Take the deputy's armed spear gun just in case."

"That confirms it," Pete countered. "You are out of your mind."

"You can't leave him in there alone, Colucci."

"Ask him to do it," Pete suggested, nodding his head towards the paramedic in the lawn chair.

"Okay, I will," Jefferson said nonchalantly, turning his head to yell at the man. "McMurphy, get your ass over here!"

The paramedic moved with the speed of a snail racing across a field of peanut butter. He shuffled more than walked, a young man, handsome with a toned body, but no piss, and apparently out of vinegar, his lumbering gate resembled an old rodeo bull rider crippled with arthritis from too many bucks and too many bad falls. Pete had never seen a man move so slowly.

Jefferson, however, knew the paramedic as one of the laziest men he'd ever known, except in an emergency. McMurphy's reputation as being slower than a stoned sloth plunged to the wayside when faced with a medical emergency. His colleagues deemed McMurphy the best paramedic on Florida's east coast. Closing the fence gate, he moseyed over to Chief Jefferson and stopped by his side, saying one word. "Yeah?"

"Glad you made the trip safely," Jefferson said, his tone laced with sarcasm. But he knew sarcasm did not affect the man. "McMurphy, you go scuba diving occasionally, right?"

"Yeah."

Jefferson gave it his best shot. "Good, that's good, McMurphy. I need you to take Colucci's equipment and...."

"Nope."

His quick refusal irritated Jefferson. "Nope? I hadn't finished asking you...."

"Nope."

"Nope, what?"

"I ain't goin' down there, that's what."

"You won't help a fellow first responder?"

"Nope."

Jefferson pointed at Pete and told McMurphy, "This old man is willing to help, but he can only do so much. If he's…"

Pete interrupted. "I'm not that old."

Jefferson countered, "Yes, you are," then returned his attention to McMurphy. "If he's willing to help, why won't you?"

"I bagged up Burke, that's why I won't help," and with that final refusal, McMurphy did what he did best unless involved with an emergency, he moseyed away. McMurphy was a feet-shuffler, but he wasn't stupid. After bagging Burke's severed body, he had no intention of being bagged himself.

"Asshole," Jefferson muttered. He looked at Pete. "You still refusing?"

"Just call me an asshole."

"Listen, Colucci. I can't make you do anything you don't…"

Pete interrupted, "Well, 'CHIEF', I guess you could give me a direct order since you swore me in as one of your deputies!"

Jefferson had been caught with his hand in a cookie jar with no cookies. Going on defense was his only option. "Well, you're fired!"

"Well, I quit!"

Both men gawked at each other, waiting for the

other fellow to blink. Pete blinked first but with a crafty smirk. Chief Jefferson snickered; Pete laughed, and Jefferson chuckled before saying, "Christ, we're the worst team in history."

"Most likely," Pete said.

Splashing water caught their attention. One diver popped up, followed by a second, neither one with their armed spear gun. Pete and Chief Jefferson thought the worst had happened, but the divers appeared indifferent as they stepped onto the bank.

Jefferson asked, "What's going on?"

LeCount, the ranking diver, responded, "We're finished down there."

Their apathetic attitude exasperated Jefferson. "Well, that is fine, just fine! But if you'd be so kind, I'd like to know where the hell Middleton is!"

LeCount knew not to push Chief Jefferson. He responded, "Oh, sorry, Chief. Well, Middleton came out of the cavern, took our spear guns, and then motioned for us to surface. We just did as we were told, but Middleton stayed at the entrance. The last I saw of him, he was aiming both spear guns at something inside the cavern, or I guess there was something inside, I don't know, I mean, we didn't see anything to be concerned about. I know you people are looking for some type of creature or something like that, but you'll have to wait for Middleton for more info."

Pete asked Jefferson, "Are you thinking what I'm thinking?"

"Yeah. Now what?" he asked Pete.

Pete asked LeCount, "You have any more armed spear guns?"

"Yeah," LeCount replied. "Two more in the car."

"Go get them, right now!" Pete blared.

With his gaze locked on the lake, Jefferson said, "Forget that."

The four men on the bank saw bubbles burst on the surface, even McMurphy arose from his patio chair throne and quick-stepped to the edge of the lake, believing he faced a second day of bagging repulsive remains. Jefferson unholstered his Glock. Snapper? Middleton? The five men had one choice: to wait.

CHAPTER 16

The five men were spooked more than anything else. Pete had seen Snapper's head, but the other four had no idea what they potentially faced, "That's got to be Middleton," Pete ventured.

"I hope so," Chief Jefferson said, his Glock clutched in his right hand, but the weapon was by his side, no aim taken. "That's a lot of bubbles."

Pete responded, "I don't think Snapper has a regulator or tanks. That's got to be Middleton," he repeated.

The few seconds they waited felt like hours. One last big burst of bubbles before Middleton resurfaced, both spear guns in his right hand, both still armed. Already near the bank, he stepped ashore quickly. Removing his mask, Middleton ordered the two other divers, "LeCount, you and Carpenter stay here. I'll be at the swamp with the other divers. When the cement trucks get here, I'll call or text you step by step. Understood?"

Both responded, "Yes, sir."

"Take the two spear guns, they're both still armed," Middleton said, handing over the weapons.

"Get your backup tanks out of the car plus the other armed spear guns. Get to it."

"Yes, sir," and both divers left.

Middleton told the paramedic, "McMurphy, you stay here. One of your coworkers will be over at the swamp, ya got it?"

"Yes, sir," and McMurphy moseyed back to the lawn chair.

Chief Jefferson finally got in a word. "Middleton, do you mind telling Colucci and me what the hell you're doing?"

"Yes, sir," Middleton said. "But our time is short, and the story is long, so save your questions until I'm finished, okay?"

Jefferson said, "Fine."

Pete said, "Sure."

Middleton began, "I reached the end of the cavern without any trouble. I never realized the swamp behind The Refuge was so big. It's huge and it's deep, more like a combination of lake and swamp. No roads, no excess that I saw, it's like virgin territory. The cavern ended about twenty feet down from the shoreline. I got out of the water and tested the ground behind the cavern. It's too soggy for cement trucks but an old dead-end road is less than sixty yards away. The cement trucks can work from there. The ground here in The Refuge is solid so the trucks will have no problem on this side of the cavern.

"My brother-in-law has his cement trucks on the way and an air-conditioning company has nine trucks on the way with hundreds of feet of commercial air-conditioning vents. We'll connect the a/c vents until they're long enough to reach the top of the mouths at both ends of the cavern then we'll pour in the cement to seal the openings. The commercial vents should be strong enough to carry the heavy cement going down. The vents curving on land into the water should handle the weight of the cement, but we can't curve the vents inside the cavern because the heavy cement would most likely split the vents apart, so we're placing the vents just above the top of the cavern to seal it from the outside. Questions?"

Chief Jefferson was impressed. "Damn, Middleton, nice job in a short time. My deputies and I will be here all…"

Pete interrupted, "Hold on a minute. We don't know if Snapper is even in the swamp."

Middleton replied, "He's there. I saw him on a far bank basking in the sun. It looked like the only place the sun gets through all the vegetation. I say 'bank', but it's a shallow spot in the water. Snapper's feet were still submerged." Middleton swallowed as he shook his head. "It's huge, the size of a lake house."

Pete wasn't convinced. "Okay, but how do you plan to entice it into the cavern?"

"Food."

"What food, you?"

"No, we're going to place a bloody cow carcass with a rope tied around it on the edge of the swamp above the cavern. When Snapper gets close enough, we'll kick the cow carcass into the water. It should sink to the entrance of the cavern or nearby. Two other divers will be with me inside the cavern, and we'll drag the carcass by the rope into the middle of the cavern and drop bloody chicken carcasses along the floor as bait."

Pete remained the devil's advocate. "What if it's not hungry, what if it's gone when you get there, what if there are fifteen other limestone caverns surrounding the swamp?"

Middleton had some of the answers. "If it's basking then it will eventually warm up and hopefully be hungry. Hell, it may not even be there when we start setting up, or it may go after the workers instead of the cow carcass, but we have to take that chance. If it spooks, we may lose it for a long time because there are several other caverns surrounding the swamp that Snapper could utilize. I noticed five in shallow water."

Jefferson spoke up. "You're counting on pure luck, Middleton, do you think this plan will work?"

"No, I don't," he replied truthfully. "It's a hope and a prayer, but if either of you have a better idea, I'll be glad to listen."

Pete suggested, "Get a Navy plane out of Jacksonville to put a cruise missile up its ass."

Middleton's answer surprised both men. "I've already thought about that. My contacts in Jacksonville said they'll get a fighter armed but don't know from which base, plus I think the higher-ups will never give authority for a Navy jet to fire a missile into a civilian area to blow up a giant turtle. It sounds ridiculous to even suggest it. Anyway, by the time a Navy jet could get here, it would be too late. I've pulled the chopper away, so the noise doesn't spook Snapper. That turtle isn't going to wait around to be blown to bits. I think my plan is the only shot we have right now."

Pete suggested, "Poison the meat."

Middleton replied, "How much poison would we need, what if Snapper doesn't take the bait, how much other wildlife would we kill, what if the poison soaked into the water system?

"Oh," Pete said.

Jefferson was encouraged. "I think it's a great plan." Jefferson teetered, almost lost his balance, and was sweating profusely. Regaining his balance, Jefferson muttered, "Damned heat."

It wasn't hot, not even warm yet. Middleton was as concerned as Pete had been. He asked Jefferson, "Are you okay?"

Jefferson replied, "Yeah, I'm fine," then quickly reverted to the task at hand. "I like your idea," he said to Middleton.

Pete didn't agree. "I think you're both bat-shit crazy. Why not dynamite the entrances?"

Middleton replied, "The swamp is a protected area, if we use dynamite the entire ecosystem may collapse plus it would take forever to get permission. If we dynamite the cavern on this end, we might collapse the cavern along with a hundred or so homes in The Refuge."

Skepticism still intact, Pete implied, "I still don't think this dog hunts."

Exasperated, Middleton countered, "I repeat, Colucci, do you have a better idea?" Pete hesitated. Middleton was finished with dissension. He raised his voice. "DO YOU?" Pete didn't reply, shrugging his shoulders as if surrendering his misgivings. Middleton continued, "Okay, things are in motion, we're not stopping." He looked at the Chief. "Chief, stay here and await my call."

"I'll be right here," Jefferson said.

Middleton looked at Pete. "You stay here, too. We may need you."

"Bullshit," Pete swore.

Middleton replied. "Bullshit back at you. Get a tank out of the patrol car and stay here with the two deputies. You've seen the turtle and you've been inside the cavern; you have just as much experience as

I do. You are part of this team whether you like it or not, DEPUTY COLUCCI. I'll be in touch." And Middleton was gone.

Pete asked Jefferson, "Who does he think he is?"

Jefferson calmly replied, "Apparently, the boss."

"This is crazy, trying to trap a turtle the size of a space shuttle inside a limestone cavern with fast-drying cement by using a cow carcass and dead chickens. Middleton doesn't even think it will work. I don't know, Chief, we may end up as Snapper's lunch."

"Well, Colucci, you may luck out, maybe Snapper doesn't like Italian food."

"Funny, Chief, real funny. There's got to be a better way."

"Could be, but we're out of... of time..." Chief Jefferson swayed like a weak palm in a hurricane, sweat poured like a waterfall from his forehead, his big bulk unbalanced, wobbling, his knees buckled. "Colucci?" he moaned for help, then collapsed, half on the bank, his upper torso in the water.

Slow-moving McMurphy was never sluggish when faced with a medical emergency. The paramedic had eyeballed Jefferson all morning. The Chief didn't look well, something was wrong. He noticed Chief Jefferson's instability, saw him swaying, and was through the fence gate and attempting to pull the Chiefs' upper torso out of the water before Pete could even react. Both men struggled to lift Jefferson's bulk out of the water and onto the bank. The Chief was still breathing but incoherent, coughing, talking nonsense. Paramedic McMurphy speculated a stroke. The two divers, LeCount and Carpenter, arrived on the scene and offered their assistance. It took all four men to manhandle Jefferson into the EMT van. McMurphy called for backup at the lake, knowing things could easily go wrong when the trapping of Snapper began, then was gone like a bat out of hell with his back tires flinging dirt and small stones onto Pete and the two divers.

LeCount was the first to speak. "What do we do now?"

Jefferson was down. Middleton had a doubtful plan in motion. Hooten, the herpetologist was missing, as were Jefferson's two deputies. LeCount asking Pete, 'What do we do now' placed Pete in a leadership role, a position he didn't seek nor want. It was a strange time to remember one of his favorite quotes, but Pete thought about the excerpt by the Count of Moncrief, *He either fears his fate too much or his desserts are small, who dares not put it to the touch, to win or lose it all.'* Inspiring little quote perhaps, but the excerpt could also apply to a Japanese kamikaze during World War II or an old man involved in police work he had no business being involved in.

LeCount pressed the issue, "What now?"

Pete replied, "We wait."

SNAPPER

* * * * *

Snapper had utilized the swamp behind The Refuse for fifteen years after his former Everglade home had been drained for a new housing project. Its new home was quiet, isolated, and blessed with an abundance of food from fish to birds to smaller turtles to wild animals stalking each other across the squelchy terrain. When Snapper craved larger meals, over a dozen wide caverns gave access to inland marshlands and lakes and deep rivers, several of the waterways leading to cattle, sheep, and horse ranches, plus dozens of farms with snacks such as pigs, goats, a pony or two. Other caverns led to several unexplored swamps and fenlands off the beaten path that offered Snapper seclusion. A missing horse, cow, or pig stirred concern about a wild animal, perchance a Black bear or Florida Panther roaming the vicinity, but not a turtle the size of a barn. Wildlife experts and no-kill trappers had been looking for the wrong predator.

Instinct kept Snapper hunting after dark and before dawn. Like all turtles, it was easily spooked during the daylight; too much noise, too many cars, and too many large worms walking about. Small worms, unattended and alone, were occasionally a part of its diet when Sniper was a youngster, but now baby worms weren't even a snack, and larger adult worms usually weren't available at night and weren't all that tasty. Their meatless shells were soft during hot cycles, thicker during cold cycles, and hard to digest. Things covering their paws were tasteless as were the occasional coverings on their heads. One big worm had fought back inside Snapper's mouth, plus used a stinger of some sort in one of its paws that exploded a hot projectile into the roof of its mouth. Unless readily available for a quick snack, Snapper avoided big worms. Not spooked; just not interested.

Adult turtles eat three or four times a week, but a cow or horse or manatee curtailed Snapper's appetite for the better part of a month. But something was stirring in its basic survival instinct, a primitive warning to depart its noisy surroundings for perhaps safer, wider open spaces with an abundance of food. Snapper had prowled such a place many times but always came 'home' to the swamps and lakes feeding into the St. Johns River. But the worms, all these walking worms, more and more inhabiting the soil around swamps and lakes and rivers, building ponds or concrete water holes by worker worms. To Snapper, survival warned of its natural surroundings fading away due to all these walking worms. The safer, wider open space with all the food availability enticed Snapper's return. The walking worms called this wide-open space the Atlantic Ocean.

CHAPTER 17

Pete and the two divers didn't have to wait long. Middleton's Navy Seal training had kicked into high gear; his organization meticulous; his orders barked with authority and no excuses or debates tolerated. Three large front discharge cement trucks had arrived across the lake. The drivers surveyed the backyards of two residents before pulling up with their heavy loads to the edge of the water over the cavern. The air-conditioning vents arrived moments later, thick, strong vents; the men hurriedly attached the industrial vents the length of the two backyards, another section to the side if needed. A stick with a red flag at the water's edge marked the middle of the cavern.

Middleton had recruited Jefferson's two deputies on his own without the approval from the Sheriff in St. John's County and without asking Chief Jefferson's permission. Middleton didn't have time for proper procedures, not that it mattered to Chief Jefferson since he'd already forfeited command to Middleton. Jefferson's deputies had witnessed the mental decline of their boss; Middleton knew the Chief was no longer the man he once was; all the omens were profound. Chief Jefferson recruited a civilian to help investigate a crime, possibly a murder or wildlife tragedy, and illegally deputized that same civilian. Jefferson's health had been declining for months, along with unpredictable behavior, sporadic slurred speech, and contradictory decisions.

Except for his spouse and younger brother, few people knew the real man, Chief Roosevelt Jefferson. His life was a closed book unless opened by the man himself, and his wife and kid brother were the only ones who understood Chief Jefferson's desperate attempt to solve the case before cancer interfered with its ugly finality. The driving force egging him on was the country girl with the gorgeous legs, the attractive undercover agent for the Florida Bureau of Investigation agent, and Pete's 'hottie' next-door neighbor, Bebi Barnes. For Jefferson, the whole incident was personal. She was Jefferson's illegitimate daughter from a fleeting rendezvous with a white cheerleader while playing football at Florida State University.

Middleton used Jefferson's two deputies to mark the cavern in The Refuge; Middleton had marked the one in the swamp. Then the two deputies knocked on every door in The Refuge to warn the residents of a 'killer alligator' in one of the lakes and to not interfere with the afternoon's activities attempting to trap or kill the beast. Residents were warned not to leave their homes except for an emergency and to bring outside pets inside. The deputies told the residents the alligator may have killed one or two humans, so the caution was proactive. The deputies also lied with the story of a possibility there may be more than one 'killer alligator'. No residents were seen all afternoon.

LeCount's cell phone chimed with the music from Lonesome Dove. He opened the right leg pocket on his diving suit, then pulled out the cell phone in a waterproof baggie. Taking it out of the baggie, he attempted to answer. "Hello? What? You're breaking up, Mike. I can't hear what you're…hello? Crap, text me!" He glanced at Pete. "It's Middleton, but he's too garbled to understand. I asked him to text me."

Pete was standing two feet from LeCount; he'd overheard the jumbled conversation, including the request for a text, but the diver appeared fidgety, perhaps still seeking leadership. Pete calmly replied, "So I heard."

Handing Pete his cell phone, LeCount said, "Here, Colucci, you take it. You and Middleton know what we're dealing with here; I don't, nor does Carpenter," he implied, nodding at his diving partner. "We will take your lead."

"Fine," Pete replied, taking the cell phone. It chimed once.

LeCount said, "That's probably Middleton."

Pete replied, "Ya think?" He read the text: *Where is Jefferson?*

Pete texted back: *Jefferson is down. Your divers taking my lead. Colucci.*

Middleton: *Down? Why?*

Pete: *Passed out, sick, on way to the hospital. Instructions?*

Frustrated, Middleton visualized his plan collapsing at the last minute and was doubtful that Pete was the man to oversee the mission in The Refuge. He texted: *Anyone else there?*

Pete: *No. Instructions?*

A long pause. Middleton was running out of time, he had to concede.

Middleton: *You do as I say, nothing else.*

Pete: *Instructions?*

Middleton: *Get down there. Crews ready to pour. You are in charge, be sure trucks dump in front of cavern, DO NOT DUMP UNTIL WE GET OUT YOUR END! Snapper awake and watching.*

Pete: *Good luck.*

Middleton: *Don't let me down!*

Pete: *Do your part, sailor; flyboy will do his.*

Handing LeCount his cell phone, Pete told him, "I don't need it anymore." He looked across the lake. The workers were fast, already sliding the long chain of vents into the water, but they had stopped sliding, no need to go deeper without the divers in position. They glanced back across the lake at the three divers as if prompting them into action, one panicky worker pointing his finger downward. Pete told LeCount and Carpenter, "Let's go."

* * * * *

Worms, more walking worms, now in its lair, noisy, clanking a long snake-like thing, shoving the noisy snake into the swamp. One worm stared back. More worms lugging a huge chunk of something, which could be meat, dropping it on the ground above one of the caverns. The curious worm kept staring as three other worms entered the water and then disappeared. The curious worm raised one of its arms then raised a smaller appendage into the air, then followed the other three worms into the water.

Warmed from basking, hungry, the walking worms still milling about on the ground would suffice as a quick snack, but they were backing away, fading into the vegetation, except for two worms standing by the chunk above the cavern. The scent of meat wafted across the swamp, it smelled like meat, it could be meat, a big meal. Snapper slid into the water to investigate.

* * * * *

Sixty yards from the cavern on a crumbling unused back road, three front-discharging cement trucks churned heavy loads in rotating mixing drums. Two waited their turn; the third truck's front discharging chute was tightly attached to the snake-like air-conditioning vents.

The driver and a coworker were inside the cab. Nervous, the driver looked at his pale coworker, "We dump in ten minutes, right?"

"Right."

"Did you see the size of that thing?"

"Yep."

"You think this will work?"

"Nope."

"I don't either. You scared?"

"Yep."

"Think those divers will be safe?"

"Nope." The coworker opened the passenger's door.

"Where are you going?"

"To take a piss."

* * * * *

The two deputies assigned to dump the bloody cow carcass into the water tentatively obeyed Middleton's direct order to 'wait until the last minute.' They watched as a turtle's carapace the size of two cement trucks headed in their direction, bobbing up and down, visible then invisible, the approaching danger giving pause for the deputies to contemplate the definition of 'the last minute.'

Deputy Deborah Newton: "I think it's close enough, don't you?"

Deputy Tommy Carter: "We were told to wait."

Newton, nervous, ready to run: "It's about forty yards away!"

Carter, macho, foolish, needing to urinate: "Wait, wait…."

Newton screamed, "Wait for what? Dump it!"

Carter, spotting his underwear: "NOW!"

Newton and Carter pushed with all their strength, the carcass rolled over; with one more push, the bloody cow splashed into the water.

Newton yelled, "RUN!" Carter hesitated as Snapper raised its huge head, not twenty yards from where he stood. The urine flowed. Frozen in fear, his life flashed before his eyes. Newton stopped running. "Damn it," she swore. She sprinted back to Carter, grabbed then pulled on his collar, screaming, "Get your ass in gear!" Carter, his pants soaked, joined his partner in a dash for their lives.

* * * * *

Snapper moved halfway out of the water as if to chase the two running worms, then suddenly stopped and watched the two worms disappear into the marshy foliage. It decided the worms weren't worth the energy. Snapper's enormous head stretched forward to sniff the long snake-like thing the worms had slipped into the water. No scent of life or meat, uninteresting. Beside the snake-like, lifeless thing, Snapper sniffed the wet soil where the big chunk had been. Blood, fresh blood, the scent of dead carrion, raw, meaty. Its primitive senses overloaded, Snapper dove for the depths.

CHAPTER 18

Having pulled the cow carcass inside the cavern, Middleton and two other divers feverishly dragged the bloody chunk of meat deeper and deeper into the limestone passageway. The fourth diver remained in front of the carcass, pulling bloody pork and raw chicken meat from a plastic bag to drop a path of smaller snacks for Snapper to follow. Mulling over the notion of being a reverse point man, the diver also chewed over the thought of being as expendable as the bloody morsels of pork and chicken. He stayed close to the cow carcass, touching the bloody meat non-stop with a fin or the back of a leg just to be sure he wasn't being served up as a sacrificial lamb.

Middleton and the other two divers had the same fear. Why in the hell were they pulling a cow carcass into a cavern in the wistful hope of trapping a giant turtle the size of a billionaire's yacht? The deeper they went and the more they thought, the harder they pulled. All the while, the fourth diver continued kicking the carcass with a fin or back leg.

The blood from the carcass filtered into the water as Middleton had hoped, deep crimson at first dwindling into a misty cloud of pink, the color of no importance but the scent being a dinner invitation.

Deeper, deeper, almost at the one slight curve near the exit to the lake. Lugging and jerking, their strength draining with each yank, but too terrified to stop. Access to the cavern from the swamp suddenly grew dim, restricting the trivial light generated by cyanobacteria, yet the visibility was not impaired enough to blind the divers. The diver with the bag of meat froze in place as his vision zeroed in on Snapper, nibbling at the tiny chunks of pork and chicken but steadily advancing in search of the bigger meal oozing blood into the cavern. Valor disappeared. Panic-stricken, the bagman diver dropped his bait and then kicked like a beaver on steroids to zoom over and beyond the three divers tugging the carcass. Aware of the diver beating a hasty retreat over their heads, Middleton and the other two deputies looked up. Snapper was less than sixty feet away from making the bloody cow carcass or them a morning meal. They dropped the rope and kicked their fins feverishly as if their lives hinged on speed, which they did. Middleton could only pray the truck drivers in the swamp had done their part and the cement was already flowing down the air-conditioning vents.

* * * * *

The driver in the cement truck hooked up to the vents pushed a button for the computer-controlled release of the cement.

Driver: "You need to be the chute man."

His coworker: "You be the chute man; I'm not going out there!"

Driver: "Somebody has to guide the chute!"

Coworker: "You idiot, the chute is attached to the vents. It ain't moving nowhere!"

Driver: "What if something goes wrong?"

Coworker: "Then it goes wrong."

Driver: "If this don't work, those divers ain't gonna make it."

Coworker: "We'll attend their funerals."

Driver: "Gezzz, are you telling me that you can live with their deaths for not watching the chute?"

Coworker: "Damn right I can."

The cement flowed, slowly at first, then picked up speed into the air-conditioning vents; the vents vibrating from the weight, sections appeared in danger of buckling but miraculously, they held. The cement soon poured like projectile vomit out of the end vent over the opening to the cavern. As advertised and as Middleton had hoped, the highly secretive military-grade rapid hardening hydraulic cement solidified in less than one minute, one truckload most likely enough to seal off the cavern, two truckloads a certainty, the third truckload for good measure. Snapper wasn't returning to the swamp.

*****

Middleton and the three deputy divers had never swum so fast in their lives, but their speed would save their hides. Snapper had gorged its feast, the tiny snacks and a large chunk of meat. Maneuvering its carapace within the confines of the cavern, it managed to reverse direction and headed back to the swamp. But something was wrong; that end of the cavern was dark, and the opening was closed by some type of stuff too hard and too thick to penetrate. Snapper backed away from the blockage, reversed course, and proceeded for the small lake at the other end of the cavern.

Pete saw the four divers frantically swimming for the opening; he knew what to do. Motioning up with his right arm, LeCount took the cue and handed Pete his armed spear gun, then kicked for the surface to signal the cement crews to start pouring the quick-hardening cement. Pete aimed both armed spear guns toward the divers, awaiting what he knew they were fleeing from. Carpenter followed suit as both men prayed the four divers would exit the cavern before Snapper rounded the slight curve in the limestone. Lady Luck favored the humans.

First Middleton, then the other three divers, exited the cavern and kicked for the surface. Pete followed, but Carpenter couldn't move, his gaze on the massive head and carapace rounding the curve and heading his way. He nervously fired the spear gun, a shot too high that sailed over Snapper's carapace to peter out without exploding.

For whatever reason, Snapper paused. Carpenter felt pressure on his right arm. It was Pete, having returned to pull Carpenter out of his trance. As he tugged on Carpenter's arm, Pete took a wild shot with his spear gun at Snapper. The spear bounced off the cavern wall, hit the other side, then exploded about twenty feet in front of Snapper. The explosion crumbled a big section of limestone. Snapper backed up, bewildered, yet knowing its only chance for escape lay ahead.

Pete and Carpenter kicked for the surface as the heavy cement poured from the vent above the cavern entrance, some hitting Carpenter's legs and knocking him downwards from the sheer weight. Pete looked back in time to witness Carpenter being entombed with cement, too heavy and too fast-drying for him to fight free. There was nothing Pete could do. Carpenter was gone, never to be recovered. Pete waited, watching tons upon tons of cement shooting from the vent, covering Carpenter and the cavern's opening. If Snapper surged through the cement before it hardened, Pete would join Carpenter wherever the unfortunate man's soul may be. He waited, accepting his fate. The cement waterfall continued, too much and hardening too quickly for Snapper to penetrate.

As Pete kicked for the surface, Snapper hesitated, then backed up, unable to comprehend that strange stuff falling in front of the cavern was sealing its fate. Pete resurfaced. Middleton and LeCount were ashore screaming at Pete to get out of the water, believing Snapper may have breached the opening before the cement had a chance to harden. Pete was too nonchalant as he came ashore; the two men grabbed his arms and pulled him forward; too many questions, too many workers hanging about for good or bad news, the second cement truck's chute already hooked up to the vents and pouring still more cement into the lake.

Middleton asked the obvious, "Where's Carpenter?"

Pete removed his mask, looked at Middleton, and pathetically replied, "Under the cement. He's gone."

LeCount muttered, "Aww, gezzzz."

Middleton couldn't accept the unacceptable. "How? What the hell happened?"

Pete's nonchalant demeanor remained intact, the result of too much death with not enough emotion to compensate; his weak voice was more of a defense mechanism than an instrument of communication. "He froze," Pete mumbled. "I tried to pull him back, but the cement hit his legs and forced him down. It was over in seconds."

Middleton swore, "Damn it!"

LeCount spoke up, "What about Snapper?"

Pete's tone didn't change, as if good news didn't counter bad news. "It's inside the cavern. We have it trapped."

CHAPTER 19

Snapper didn't like being trapped, and it didn't like the fading light. The closures dimmed the natural light, which routinely facilitated the cyanobacteria to photo-synthesize. Instinct and survival create a happy marriage.

Snapper lingered beside the long crevice Pete had investigated with his flashlight. Wide enough for Snapper to enter, except for the height. Snapper stuck its head in with ease, but its huge carapace thudded into the limestone above the crevice, and its thick legs were unable to squeeze inside. It pounded against the limestone. The limestone held. Snapper backed off; its eyes zeroed in on the impediment. Brute force, escape, or death; its only two options. Snapper retracted its head and surged forth, slamming its massive bulk into the crevice. The limestone held. Snapper pulled back for another attempt.

* * * * *

Above ground, the men felt a slight tremor, followed by one more, then another, then another. Pete asked, "Do you guys feel that?"

Middleton guessed correctly, "That's Snapper."

LeCount asked worriedly, "Doing what?"

Middleton guessed incorrectly, "It's butting the cement, trying to escape."

Pete asked, "Will the concrete hold?"

Middleton replied, "It will hold, that damn stuff could hold back a locomotive."

Stronger tremors, weaker tremors, no tremors at all. The men waited and waited and waited some more.

Pete spoke first. "Think it's given up?"

Middleton replied, "It's done for, probably broke its neck."

Middleton was wrong; Snapper had broken out.

* * * * *

The timeworn limestone was too porous to impede continued assaults by a five-ton turtle. The cracks formed after Snapper battered the crevice twelve times; its next charge crumbled a section of cavern wall; its last onslaught carved the limestone into an opening large enough for Snapper to enter the grotto. All was quiet inside the blocked-off cavern and would be for eternity.

Snapper began a new exploration, weaving through unknown territory, scraping the limestone sides, forcing its way through thinner paths of soft minerals, maneuvering methodically in the darkness, all its instincts guiding its mass forward. The smells, small schools of fish coming and going indicated a well-used aquatic highway. The grotto narrowed, then widened, and took a sharp turn upward, exposing a faint light ahead. Snapper was energized, moving faster and faster towards the light, a light becoming brighter and brighter, a large opening, an easy exit; Snapper emerged in the St. Johns River between the Saturiwa and Deep Creek Conservation Areas.

Exposing nostrils for oxygen and eyes for surveillance, Snapper kept low, exhausted, frightened beyond cautious, not wanting any contact with more worms. Two sailboats sailed mid-river, ski-boats zipped across the water pulling worms holding ropes while standing on wooden sticks, as other worms sat immobile in smaller things nearer shore holding sticks with strings dipped in the water.

All the activity came from the Riverdale Park and Boat Ramp, a quarter mile north of where Snapper rested. A pontoon boat puttered into view, slowed, then stopped. Big worms, three smaller worms, and a wrinkled worm jumped into the water, splashing and yelling as if inviting Snapper to dinner. The big chunk of meat inside the cavern and the smaller snacks had satisfied its hunger, but survival was still in question.

These worms, all these worms, some an easy catch, most not worth the effort. Smart worms had threatened to terminate Snapper's existence inside the cavern, and more worms were pushing into shelters and swamps and lakes and ponds and rivers to construct nests of wood and stone and hard materials. Too many busy worms, too much noise, and too much nature vanishing day by day.

Snapper's hunting grounds, its safe areas from the noise and invading worms all but gone, the predator now the hunted, it was time to return to the big salty lake, a lake with unlimited food, shelter, and safety. Snapper dove as deep as the St. John's River allowed and began its long journey, past Green Cove, Fruit Cove, Orange Park, and the Jacksonville Naval Air Station. Slowing for the narrow channel around Jacksonville, too many worms on the water, too much activity and noise, always the noise. Around Reddie Point, past Blount Island, dodging commercial worm boats bigger than itself, then past NAS Mayport and into the huge salty lake, never to return to rivers and lakes and swamps and ponds, too much noise, too much danger, too many worms.

* * * * *

After the day's horrendous events, the clean-up in The Refuge and the neighboring swamp seemed anticlimactic. Emotions ran amuck: relief that Snapper had been contained, sadness over the death of Carpenter, and disbelief that it was all over. Even Middleton was shocked that his plan had worked. The cement and air-conditioning crews had tidied up the two areas, packed up chutes and vents and tools, and wondered how to tell family and friends what they had experienced, yet doubted the acceptance of their stories. The crews weren't debriefed nor told what or what not to say but did appreciate the 'job well done' from Pete and the deputy divers.

Middleton had tons of reports to fill out, including a statement from Pete concerning Carpenter's death. The thought of their friend and coworker buried under tons of concrete dampened any celebration of success. Pete and Middleton had shaken hands, complimented each other's contributions, and enjoyed the only humorous moment when Middleton advised Pete to retire from police work. Pete managed a frivolous grin before concurring.

The deputies piled into two patrol cars and headed for a sense of normalcy at the Sheriff's Department. The two paramedics had accepted an emergency dispatch and pulled out early on. Pete went home to change from a wet suit into decent summer attire to visit Chief Jefferson, who had been admitted to Flagler Hospital. Life had returned to ordinary. It all seemed so boring.

CHAPTER 20

Pete thumbed through a copy of Florida's Habitat while sitting in the Critical Care Unit's waiting room at Flagler Hospital. He wasn't allowed to visit Chief Jefferson since Jefferson's family had been called in. Jefferson's medical condition was worse than anyone had suspected, except for the man entering the waiting room.

Tall, skinny, shiny black skin, thin face with too many wrinkles from too many years in Oncology. "Are you Mister Colucci," he asked Pete.

Pete stood up. "Yes, sir."

He offered Pete his hand, "I'm Doctor Lincoln Jefferson, my brother's Oncologist."

"My pleasure, sir," Pete said. They broke the handshake. "How is…."

Doctor Lincoln Jefferson interrupted, "Sit down, Mister Colucci, and let's talk." Both sat down, one chair separating them. "As you may have guessed from my first name, our mother was a self-taught Presidential historian."

Pete grinned. "I can see that."

Doctor Jefferson informed Pete, "Mister Colucci, my brother has passed."

That was news Pete hadn't prepared for. Stunned, Pete said, "I hate to hear that. I had no idea he was that close to… well, you know."

"I was the only one who knew, Mister Colucci. My brother was functioning on heavy narcotics, some prescribed, others under the counter." He stopped for Pete's reaction.

Under the counter, a brother for an Oncologist; Pete grasped the meaning. "I understand, sir."

Doctor Jefferson continued. "Mister Colucci, my brother was not functioning normally for at least a month, but he wouldn't give up, he wouldn't give in. He was that way his entire life. As kids, he was the bulk, and I was the brain. If skinny me got in trouble or was picked on, Roosevelt was always there to solve the problem with or without his fists. I wanted to be a doctor, and he wanted to be a professional football player. The scouts had been watching him from high school to college until a knee injury killed his dream of a professional career with the Green Bay Packers, his favorite team. He worshiped their legendary coach, Vince Lombardi. Roosevelt's career in law enforcement only paid the bills."

Pete spoke up. "He was a good cop."

Doctor Jefferson chuckled. "Well, if you say so. Roosevelt was brutal at times, lessons well learned during segregation, but he kept the peace. He didn't care about popularity; he understood that respect generated results. Every cop and crook in Florida avoided trouble in New St. Francis, and I suppose in a primitive way, perhaps the fear of law is a good thing."

Doctor Jefferson leaned forward in his chair. "Roosevelt told me about you, sir, recruiting your help, illegally deputizing you, something he would have never done until falling into the hell of narcotics that killed his pain. His thought process and decisions were warped, to say the least. I'm not belittling your contribution; I'm saying it never would have happened if Roosevelt had been in his right mind."

Pete conceded the truth. "I understand."

Changing the subject, Doctor Jefferson asked, "This animal you people were after, a giant turtle according to Roosevelt, have you had any luck dealing with…."

Pete interrupted, "We have it trapped in an underwater cavern; it's done for."

Sitting back in his chair, the doctor stated, "Roosevelt would've been very happy about that, especially after losing his daughter to it."

Another stunning moment for Pete. "What daughter?"

"Bebi Barnes. I think she was your neighbor."

"She was his daughter?" Pete replied, having trouble accepting all the twists and turns he'd been exposed to while attempting to help slay a five-ton turtle."

"Yes, sir. Out of wedlock from, let's say, a mistake he made in college. Roosevelt had a brief tryst with a white cheerleader at Florida State, and Bebi was the result. Roosevelt wanted to do the right thing, but the mother refused marriage, knowing their tryst wasn't based on love.

"Bebi's mother was a wonderful girl, loving and intelligent. She eventually earned a master's degree in Native American History. She named her newborn Bebi after a Creek lullaby called Baby Sleep, Bebi meaning baby. She taught history until she lost her life in a car accident a few years back. I know that Roosevelt loved Bebi; he provided the mother with funds that she never asked for, but they worked together to provide for Bebi as best they could.

"Roosevelt and Bebi had a great relationship, but only his wife and I knew the truth. He was crushed by Bebi's death and over-anxious to solve the case before cancer took him to the other side."

"I didn't know," Pete said, softly. "She was a beautiful young lady."

"That she was," Doctor Jefferson replied. "The turtle that was trapped, how big was it?"

"We're guessing around five tons."

Doctor Jefferson was stunned. "Five tons?"

"Afraid so."

"Humm, I guess that will be the lead on the six o'clock news."

"We hope not. Anyone in authority is lying like crazy, trying to prevent a public panic. If the truth got out, we'd have major networks warping the facts, conspiracy freaks; I mean, who will believe us without any evidence?"

"I see your point." Doctor Jefferson stood up and offered his hand for a parting handshake. Pete stood up and accepted. "It's been a pleasure talking to you, Mister Colucci. I wish you the best of luck and health."

Pete broke the handshake. "My health is good, Doc, but after all this, well, I think my mental health may be in question."

Both men chuckled. The doc said, "Goodbye, Mister Colucci."

"Goodbye, sir, please give my condolences to the family."

"I will."

* * * * *

Pete took the elevator to the main floor and started sauntering indifferently across the lobby, deep in thought, not watching where he walked, nor did he care. His head was bowed, his brain filled with images of Bebi Barnes, the Chief, Snapper, a deputy bitten in half and another one entombed in concrete, his daughter Lisa and how to explain what happened after she left for Atlanta, and Middleton, the driving force behind the demise of a killer turtle. A killer turtle. He still scoffed at the irony, the insinuation, the horror of it all.

"Colucci?"

Startled, Pete stopped and looked up. He'd come face to face with Middleton. "You woke me up, Middleton. I was deep in thought."

"You looked like it," Middleton agreed.

Pete said, "So, what's up?"

"I came to check on the Chief. How is he?"

"Gone."

"What?"

"The Chief was a lot sicker than we thought, pretty much on his death bed but trying to function on narcotics his brother gave him for pain. I met his brother in the waiting room; he told me the story."

Sagging his shoulders, briefly shaking his head, Middleton said, "We've lost a lot of good people in the past few days."

"That we have."

Middleton informed Pete, "The Sheriff is leaving his conference in New Orleans and will be back late tonight. He commended me over the phone, but I don't know if he believed me. When you think about it, Colucci, it all sounds so crazy. A people-eating turtle? We are putting a major 'spin' on this story unless we want a statewide panic, or more likely, a one-way ticket to the nuthouse."

"I don't want a repeat; I can tell you that," Pete said, noticing a familiar face walking up behind Middleton. Pete asked, "Where in the hell have you been?"

The herpetologist from the University of Florida, Ron Hooten, greeted the two men, "Gentlemen."

Pete said, "I repeat, where have you been?"

"In Gainesville. My fellow professors and I have been debating, well, let's say arguing, over what may be in the water system around here. We had two Zoom conference meetings with every prominent herpetologist in the world. Our main source of identification was the feces found behind your house, Mister Colucci. After extensive and intensive analysis, a slight majority of my colleagues and I believe this beast could fall within the classification of an Archelon. If not, then perhaps within the excepted family tree of Protostegidae. Some cells indicated a trace of Alligator Snapping Turtle, but the exact classification defies our…"

Middleton had heard enough speculation and not enough facts. He interrupted, "In other words, we still don't know what we've trapped, right?"

"I heard about the trapping," Hooten said. "I tried to call Chief Jefferson but could only leave a message, then I texted, still no reply. I dropped by the police station, and one of his deputies told me about trapping Snapper and about Jefferson being in the hospital. How's he doing?"

Pete replied, "I don't think his deputies, or the residents of New St. Francis, have been informed yet, but Jefferson has passed."

"Oh," Hooten softly replied. "I hate to hear that. I liked Chief Jefferson."

Middleton said, "He was one of a kind, that's for sure. Hooten, do you have anything else for us?"

"Well, how much concrete is holding back Snapper?"

"Plenty. Why?"

"At some point in the future, Snapper will starve to death, after which we would like to drill through the concrete to retrieve its remains for further study."

Pete jumped in, "Good luck with that!"

Middleton confirmed, "You'll play hell getting permission to do that."

Hooten tried to explain the reason. "Gentlemen, we must be sure of our analysis on the…."

Middleton was losing his patience, "Sure of what, Hooten? It sounds like you're not sure of anything."

"Agreed," Hooten replied. "We're not sure of its classification, but we would like to confirm our speculation on its age."

"Why?" Pete asked.

"Mister Colucci, we are fairly sure that Snapper is a youngster, basically a toddler turtle."

"Middleton raised his voice, "WHAT?"

"It may have been a hundred years old for all we

know, but the cell structure indicates it's still growing. Snapper is a teenager."

Unable to absorb the information, Pete stuttered, "Wait... wait just a second here. I mean if it's a 'teenager' as you speculate, then where are mom and dad?"

Hooten remained matter-of-factly, "They'd be too big for lakes and rivers, we're guessing they're in the ocean, only coming up for air, then diving and staying deep for prey large enough for a meal. Turtles spook easy, even big ones."

Middleton couldn't believe what he heard. "Are you telling us that turtles bigger than Snapper could one day crawl up on our beaches for a snack?"

Hooten told the un-Godly truth. "No, we don't think the bigger turtles will ever come ashore here. They probably nest and rest on a remote island somewhere to avoid contact with a species more dangerous than they are: the human species. The thing we're most worried about is Snapper's siblings, its brothers and sisters."

Pete looked at Middleton; Middleton stared back, both horror-struck and getting sick to their stomachs.

CHAPTER 21:
THE BROOD ON THE BEACH

Nearly a year had passed. Among the spin, cover-ups, tabloid articles, denials, true accounts of Snapper sounding like alien abductions, and the mainstream media and podcasters having lost interest in what used to be an audience-catching if not a comical story of a turtle the size of a beach house, ordinary life had returned to New St. Francis and the business and housing building boom in St. Augustine continued unabated.

Pete had sold his overpriced property to a New York replant for a sizable sum of money and moved back to Atlanta to help his daughter, Lisa, with her male enhancement business while working on a new fiction book entitled *Snapper*.

The St. Augustine sheriff had retired; Middleton decided not to retire and was elected as St. Augustine's new sheriff. Always in the back of his mind was Snapper, its sibling rivals, and mom and pop Snapper out there in the Atlantic, somewhere, hiding and feeding, shunning the noisy hustle and bustle of civilization, but for how long?

As time marched forward, his concern faded, yet

the nightmares continued, of Burke being bitten into two pieces and of Carpenter being entombed under tons of cement. Middleton had a framed excerpt by Sophocles hanging on the wall behind his sheriff's desk: *Time is a kindly God.* Feasibly, but for a cursed few, time can be ungodly.

A political issue now dominated the headlines concerning an environmental disaster off the northeast coast of Florida. A fully loaded oil tanker had caught fire after a serious explosion in the engine room. The crew abandoned the ship too soon, too scared to fight the flames, too concerned about their hides instead of preventing the largest oil spill in America's long dependency on fossil fuels. Ten miles out to sea, an enormous oil slick moved with the tide toward the pristine beaches from Jacksonville down to Cape Canaveral.

The response to contain the oil slick gained worldwide praise as the United States, Canada, Central and South American nations along with a few European countries pooled their resources to prevent the famous beaches from ruin. Their amazing success, however, didn't satisfy hordes of climate change activists and environmental warriors clogging beaches with protest signs and litter. Tourism nose-dived, yet motels and hotels remained at full occupancy with dissenters, news reporters, clean-up crews, and government representatives from every agency claiming to be making a worthwhile contribution.

The disaster at sea had triggered an economic bonanza for businesses, restaurants, fast food joints, motels, and hotels along with thousands of parking tickets and taxes streaming into government coffers. College students and beach bums staggered in and out of nightclubs and bars, not out of philosophical concern for the beaches or a possible environmental disaster, but taking advantage of a new opportunity to party hard.

Herpetologist Ron Hooten, his wife, and their three offspring were in St. Augustine for a working vacation. Hooten's worry centered on the environmental damage the oil slick may have on the reptile population, both on land and in water. So far, so good, no ongoing disruption in the reptile community, but local deep-sea fishing charters, shrimpers, and ski-jet rentals were going broke. The oil spill wreaked mayhem on the sea's food chain. Billions of small fish were dead, and the bigger fish left for cleaner hunting grounds, as did the waterfowl. Very few predators remained.

A blisteringly hot day. The Hooten family kept cool under the St. Augustine pier. The kids dug up wet sand with their plastic shovels, dumped the sand into plastic buckets, dumped the buckets when full, and kept on digging. Hooten and his wife relaxed in beach chairs while sipping on cold margaritas from their purple Yeti cooler. Unconcerned with a beach full of loud protestors being baked beet red by the sun, Hooten overheard two activists just a few feet away. They held their protest signs upside down, the top of the wood stick sticking into the sand, a male pointing out to sea, the female straining her eyes. Hooten heard them mention, 'submarine' and 'conning tower' and 'I'm not sure'.

Finishing his margarita, Hooten got out of his beach chair, told his wife, "Be right back," and then ambled nonchalantly over to the couple. Out of nothing more than boredom and curiosity, he asked, "What are you two good people looking at?"

The male replied, "I don't know, man, it looks like the conning tower of a submarine."

The female said, "I don't think it's a submarine. Look! There's another one."

Hooten had trouble focusing on the objects, the morning sun's bright rays reflecting off the ocean, briefly restricting his vision. "Where?" he asked, placing his right hand over his eyebrows to hopefully shade the brightness.

The male pointed at the end of the pier. "Right there, past the pier about a hundred yards or so. Another one's to the right."

The female became giddy with excitement, not understanding what was popping up, not knowing the congested beach could pass for a gathering of large worms. "Look! There's another one!" Two more popped up. "Holy shit, they're popping up like popcorn," she commented. Three more conning towers popped up.

Hooten's vision finally focused on the conning towers moving slowly in the direction of the beach. He swallowed hard before muttering, "Dear God, help us."